SAVED BY THE HEADLESS HORSEMAN

A MONSTROUS HOLIDAY SERIES
BOOK 3

CHARLOTTE SWAN

This is a work of fiction. Names, characters, places, and incidents either are the product of the author's imagination or are used fictitiously. Any resemblance to actual persons, living or dead, events, or locales is entirely coincidental.

Copyright © 2025 by Charlotte Swan

All rights reserved. No part of this book may be reproduced or used in any manner without the written permission of the copyright owner, except for the use of quotations in a book review. For more information, address: authorcharlotteswan@gmail.com.

eBook ISBN: 978-1-960615-15-2

Paperback ISBN: 978-1-960615-16-9

Cover Design by Charlotte Swan

www.authorcharlotteswan.com

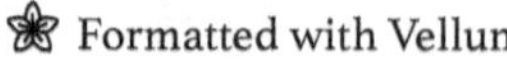 Formatted with Vellum

For those of you who believe love is stronger than death...

AUTHOR'S NOTE

This book tackles themes of depression, suicidal thoughts, and ideation. There is also a mention and description of self-harm in the form of injury (off-page flashback) and starvation. If you find these topics triggering or upsetting in any way, please refrain from continuing further in the book.

If you or someone you know is struggling with their mental health, please know you are not alone.

If you are suicidal or in emotional distress, consider using the 988 Suicide & Crisis Lifeline.

Call or text 988 or start a chat online to connect with a trained crisis counselor. The Lifeline provides 24-hour, confidential support to anyone in suicidal crisis or emotional distress.

For a full list of TW/CW visit my website www.authorcharlotteswan.com.

1

———

SCARLETT

y hand is steady as I copy the four simple lines. The black ink against the parchment creates a stark contrast. Despite my careful precision, the words are anything but unique. I have spent the last month writing down the same sentences and matching my mother's script exactly.

No doubt she'll find errors in my work—she always does.

At one point, her displeasure would've meant something to me. I would've been eager to please and beg for a chance to correct my mistake. That is not the case now. I can see these words when I close my eyes at night. They torment me when sleep will not come. It's been at least a month since I slept longer than a few fitful hours.

I dip my pen into the ink pot and start on the third line. This task is mundane and surely does not require so many of my father's guards. However, they aren't here to observe my penmanship. They are here to make sure I don't throw open the stained-glass windows inside the study and fling myself out of them. Tumbling down onto the overgrown lawn below and falling into a puzzle of broken limbs, never to be put back together again.

Or perhaps they worry I'll try to flee again, though I can assure them there is no risk of that. Once I saw the body, I had no desire ever to set foot into the *Whispering Woods* again.

It is not out of parental concern that my father has his men stationed in here. No, these guards are here to ensure I will make it to tomorrow evening. Once I am wed and the duke's gold fills my father's coffers, my father will no longer be my warden. I will be free to do as I please.

And if that means ending up broken along the cliffs of Darkwood Castle, then so be it.

My father will not shed a single tear. Come tomorrow, I will be the Duke of Greenbooke and his son, Bram's problem—a problem they won't have to stomach for long.

A familiar numbness settles inside me. Ice encases my body, weakening my hand. It falls limply to the table, still clutching the pen. I don't know how I've lasted this long—it hasn't been for lack of trying.

I would've starved myself to death weeks ago if my mother's servants had not begun force-feeding me some vile concoction. It tastes like rotten eggs and smells even worse, but it keeps me alive. As such, it is forced down my throat every morning despite my protests. While it may keep me from death, I'm not immune to the effect not eating has had on my body.

Bathing is another forced task, and once the servants have scrubbed me pink, I stand before the mirror, not recognizing the creature staring back at me. Her long, pale, blonde hair hangs limply down her back. Each one of her ribs pokes from beneath her sallow skin like the roots of a tree sprouting through the soil. Sharp cheeks and gaunt eyes make me look every bit the wraith I feel like. Cursed to live but wishing for death, stuck in this infernal realm alone.

He used to call me his moon—luminous and glowing—and

he was my sun. The two of us are opposites, yet the same. In the night, hidden by darkness, is where we would converge, becoming one after spending the day separated. Our fates were woven together by the same magic that made the stars.

Now there is nothing. Only an unending emptiness fills my lungs with broken glass. My heart bleeds inside my chest, its pounding irregularly as if still searching for the one it was tied to. There is a void that stretches, consuming everything in its path. My only consolation is knowing that tomorrow this will all be over.

I will only be an earl's wife for a moment. Scoffing at the idea, one of the guards looks up, not used to my uttering a sound during the hours spent locked inside here. I stare back at him, and the blankness in my gaze causes him to avert his eyes. I am a creature to them—they can't understand why I would let this twist me. They think I should be grateful to the duke and his son.

They will be lucky if I do not drag both of them into death with me. That is what they deserve for what they did. There is only one whom I call husband—once I am no more will be reunited. Our vows of eternity will see our souls entwined in whatever world lies beyond this one.

Our stolen nights are the only thing I hold dear. Beneath the moon, we laid ourselves bare and made promises of forever. Whispered confessions and stifled sighs with only the stars as our witnesses. I should've known it wasn't going to last. We had gotten so close to having it all—at least I believed we had. What a fool I was to not see things for what they were.

If only I had been more careful and fled Crow's Claw Manor while we still had a chance, everything would be different. Especially if he had not—

My eyes burn, but no tears fall. I've used them all up over this past month. My hand trembles as it grips the pen. The last line is pristine save for the final letter. A sharp jerk and a droplet of dark ink blights the perfect replication. It runs down the paper in a steady stream, collecting at the edge.

The page may weep, but I cannot. Returning the pen to the ink pot, I sit back against the stiff chair. My corset is too big, making it so my mother's ladies have to lace me into it twice as tightly. It is an effort to even lift my hand and add this page of vows to the already high stack. I would hide the offending note from my mother if I feared her punishment.

However, there is nothing she can do to me now that would be worse than the hell I'm living in. What can you be threatened with when you've already lost everything? My hands begin to shake violently atop the table until I'm forced to clutch them in my lap. Whether the trembling is from insomnia, hunger, pain, or a bleak combination of all three, I cannot be sure.

My hands flatten along the skirt of my dark gown. It won't be long now.

As if on cue, the midday bells chime from the clock tower above. The harsh bells ring out and add to the pounding in my head. I remain perfectly still as the study door is pulled open. The quick, steady click of my mother's elegant gait echoes on the stone floor behind me. Before this month, I would've risen from my seat and bowed to my lady mother as was her due as an earl's wife.

Now, Countess Christina will have to do without my flattery.

I was a fool to think playing the part of a perfect daughter would've earned me at least her favor. I had done everything that was asked of me without complaint. We had both done what was demanded of us in the hopes of one day being rewarded, or at the very least given our freedom to make our own way. I should've known better.

From the moment I was born and pronounced a girl, my only value became that of a bargaining chip. A prized mare to be sold off to the highest bidder who could expand my father's lands and wealth. His ambition has taken everything from me. That is why I stare blankly ahead even as my mother drifts into view.

Storm clouds roll in over the rocky shore. The sky is a pale gray as if it, too, is in mourning.

My mother stops above me, ever the foreboding finger. Her gray hair is pulled into a tight twist at the back of her head. She was still a beauty, even with the deep wrinkles around the pale blue eyes she gave me. Her red lips were already pinched in disapproval. She doesn't understand. Her marriage to my father was out of necessity, not love. If she cares about the current decline in my appearance, she doesn't show it.

There had only been one time when her mask had slipped. The night she found me in the bath, surrounded by crimson water, a jagged piece of glass clutched tightly in my hand. For a moment, she had been a concerned mother, but that worry had faded faster than the scars on my wrists.

After that night, my parents started being more careful. This was not some heartache I would recover from. I longed for a more permanent solution and therefore needed to be overseen.

This marriage had already cost them enough. If I did not make it down the aisle, it would all be for not.

My mother lifts the stack of papers. The weeping one rests at the top. She lifts it towards the fading light from the window as her lips twist—a sound of disapproval seeps from her open mouth. Thumbing through the others quickly, I stare blankly ahead. I must look like all the other ghosts that haunt this manor home.

If my soul is damned to fester behind these walls, I can only pray that he will join me here. I will not hold my breath; it seems none of my prayers are to be answered.

"Almost perfect," my mother sighs.

I say nothing, merely watch thick raindrops race along the window pane. From the corner of my eye, I watch my mother's lips flatten—her whole body jerks with the force of her sigh.

"Nothing can be done now. Accept it."

That breaks me from my despair momentarily. My eyes lift and meet her matching blue gaze. Whatever she beholds in my eyes causes fear to overtake her countenance. It is not enough to bring a smile to my lips, but satisfaction does slither along my spine.

Countess Christian doesn't recognize the creature she helped create. That is why she doesn't care what becomes of Scarlett, the perfect daughter she once had. The one she doted on as a child, the one she helped rear into the perfect lady— her only child. That girl is already dead. She died in the *Whispering Woods* alongside him.

The earl's dagger had ended two lives that night.

"Come."

Mother's words are as sharp as a whip as she looks away. I make no move to get up. I don't have to. The cold hands of my mother's ladies-in-waiting snatch me from the high-backed wooden chair. The legs scrape harshly along the stone floor.

I don't fight them anymore; it would do me little good. I let them drag me from the study. My slipper-clad feet slide along the floors. The bodice of my dress hangs limply from my shoulders. All my clothes are too big for my new body.

Portraits of the Crest family decorate the stone walls. They are the only witnesses to my harsh handling. I wonder what they think of us—of what has become of their noble bloodline. My father is from a long line of earls who have lorded over Broken Cliff. Our family had been some of the first settlers to make landfall here after navigating the rough shores.

There are hundreds of years of our history stored away in this manor. Tales of adventurous men and judicious rulers that made Broken Cliff prosper. Now there was only my father, and all of this would end with him—the last in a long line of men who had been able to father dozens of sons. My grandfather had only managed two, and one died in infancy.

My father had not even been lucky enough for any of my would-be brothers to take their first breath. Perhaps a curse was laid on our family years ago. Our fates had already been chosen, and we would find our end at the hands of greed. All of my father's ambitions have led to our end. How much blood needed to be spilled to save this crumbling manor home, only to have no one to inherit it upon his death?

Perhaps my father believes I will bear Earl Bram's sons and one of them will become his heir. I will have no children, least of all the earl's, not after what he has done. It would be justified to wrap my arms around him and leap from the cliff, dragging him down with me onto the rocky shore.

It would be fair for him to know only pain in his final moments.

The doors to my bedroom are pulled open. A great groan echoes down the hall as I'm quickly hauled inside. The room is empty save for a small mattress on the floor and a sheet barely large enough to cover me at night. They don't trust me with much else. The bars on my windows are a testament to that.

In the center of the room is an older woman, her red hair graying at the temples. Pins pierce through her apron, and a soft measuring tape hangs around her neck. The town seamstress says nothing, blanketing her expression with only the slightest widening of her eyes, the only hint that my form is a distressing sight. A white gang hangs from her arms, and my stomach rolls.

The doors to the room slam shut. Metallic clanking from the other side echoes as the guards take their place outside the door.

My mother snaps her fingers, and without preamble, her servants undress me. It takes barely a tug for the loose dress to flutter to the ground. My corset and shift follow until I am bare before all those gathered. There would've been a time when I would've covered myself in the name of modesty. I feel nothing as they look at me.

The gaunt state of my body is a physical reminder of all they have taken from me. Part of me aches at the notion that the body he once loved so fiercely is no more. All that remains is dry skin and protruding bones. My body is a coffin, housing the heart that died loving him.

"Dress her," my mother commands.

Her words wake the seamstress from her shock-induced stupor. Quickly, she gets to work sliding the white monstrosity over my slight frame. White gauze caresses my skin, making my stomach roll. Nausea creeps up my throat, coating my tongue in bile. The lacing at the back is done up, but the gown still gapes at my hips and chest.

This dress will become my death shroud. It hangs limply from my shoulders. The seamstress steps back, looking nervous —my mother's stony face twists with displeasure.

"We'll need to take it in again. She's thinner than before."

The seamstress's voice is barely above a whisper. My mother gives a sharp nod.

"Whatever is needed to make it fit. Double corset her if need be. The Duke cannot know the state we are delivering her in."

The seamstress suggests adding padding to certain areas of my body, and my mother agrees. The two make a plan in hushed tones about where to add volume and where to add color to my face to give the appearance of health. Their voices fade into the background as I stare out my window. The cold, gray sky adds more raindrops to the glass.

Sometimes, I think I can see him. Whether it is a vivid memory or pure hallucination, I cannot be certain. There will be a certain shape to the clouds that will remind me of his smile. At night, I can hear his soft voice whispering in my ear. I can feel the phantom touches of his fingers along my skin, only for my hands to be greeted by nothingness.

This pain will end soon. I hope that wherever my soul goes, he will already be waiting for me. Our reunion will be as sweet as I've imagined it to be a hundred times. Tomorrow will be my final sunrise. At dusk, I will marry Earl Bram—the man who took everything from me.

With my last breath, I will say my wedding vows, and then it will all be over. Death beckons me into its waiting embrace, and I shall not deny the two of us any longer.

2

THE HEADLESS HORSEMAN

The first day was agony.

His pain was intense enough to blight his sight and steal his breath. The fire had ravaged his body, leaving behind blistered skin and broken bones. What he had once been was gone. His memories were faded—only brief snippets of visions and the whisper of voices. They beseeched him to remember who he was. Each one that followed was weaker, a fragment of a forgotten dream.

Who he had once been was sacrificed to the being he became. A creature spawned inside that forsaken world. His only motivation was to inflict pain and suffering on the world that had been cruel to him.

At first, when he tried to stand, his legs would buckle and snap. The muscles and tendons would grow slowly back together. Bone would reform and become hardened. As he lay wallowing in his pain, the vision became clearer. It was on the fifth day that he remembered where he was.

The *Whispering Woods*—the last place he had set foot before—

More staggering pain had rocked through him. This time it

wasn't just physical. Memories came rushing back in a tangled jumble. Each one more devastating than the last. He saw what he had had. How he had come so close to getting everything before it all was ripped away.

He was merely a shivering husk where his body should be. Pain lacerated it from every angle. He was alone in the dark forest. In those dark hours, he only thought of one thing, even if it brought him more pain to do so. He couldn't help himself; he never could.

It was at least a week before he was able to rise on new legs. They supported him this time, and he stumbled through the dimly lit woods. Tripping over overgrown roots and sliding on leaf litter, he finally made his way to a stream.

The first glimpse of his reflection nearly stopped his heart. The truth of what he had become was too much to bear. That is when he screamed and screamed. The happiness of having his voice back was short-lived. The sight of him now was a gruesome one.

He was a monster—an unholy legend.

Madness set in next; that was the only explanation. As his power grew, he began to understand this new form and the magic it brought. Every day that passed, his determination grew. His memories were back, and he remembered everything. He spent weeks understanding what was done to him. It had been one final kindness to be given this form so that he might impart his revenge on those responsible.

He was a thing of myth and shadow. Those stories meant to frighten young children would now be his weapon. Each day he remembered, and each day he made plans. Determined to get revenge on the ones who cursed him with this existence. It was clear what had brought him back—the rage and need for revenge. He would see justice served to all of them.

Wandering through the forest, he came upon a large glowing pumpkin. He nearly laughed at fate's cruel joke. Lifting it from the ground, he placed it upon his bare shoulders. Green fire kindled and spread, forging eye and mouth holes. Snapping flames spilt from the openings, and he could see with shocking clarity.

He laughed again, though nothing was amusing. He had become the very beast he had been sent to kill. The imprint of the knife in his back lingered like a phantom pain.

The moon glowed above him, reminding him of her. He quickly shook himself. She was just as guilty as the rest of them. Even if his heart still beat for her, he could not deny her treachery—the part she played in all of this. His plan had to be decisive and quick.

What was certain was that they would all meet their demise at his hand. He would ensure that each one suffered the way that he had in the end, all but her.

For her, he had something far more painful in mind. He would take his time with her, ensuring she felt as hopeless as he did at the end. She would confess her betrayal, and then—and only then—would he give her the relief she sought.

In death.

3

———

SCARLETT

Gray water batters the rocky shore below.

Large swells hit the sides of the cliffs with loud, thunderous claps. Overhead, heavy rain clouds pollute the sky. The sun will not appear for this union today.

Jagged rocks stretch up between the waves like fingers, urging me towards them. The only thing preventing me from jumping into their outstretched hands is my father's iron grip on my arm. Dressed in his finery, the golden buttons of his jacket sparkle. His leather shoes have been meticulously polished. Earl Richard will always be a vain man. His unrelenting conceit drips from every line of his body.

My mother remains on my other side as stiff as a board. There is a paleness in her cheeks that I haven't seen in some time. Her steely blue eyes remain forward as she stays silent. There are no words of encouragement to be bestowed on her only daughter's wedding day. No discussion of what to expect inside my wedding bed. Though there was no need for that, Earl Bram was not receiving the virgin bride he was promised.

Nor did I have any intention of making it that far into our union.

The white gown I had been forced into was adorned with lace and satin. Delicate sleeves encased my arms, hiding any previous injuries and just how frail I'd become. Just as the seamstress had suggested, padding had been added along my hips and chest, giving the illusion of the figure I once had. The double corset I had on was nearly rib-breaking, but I managed with shallow breaths.

The pain barely registered as it complemented the perpetual hell I have been in. One final insult was laid when a bow was tied around my neck as if encasing a lamb you intended to slaughter in wrapping paper. I was not a gift to the duke and his son. I was a means to an end.

I keep my head straight as we walk the short distance to meet my betrothed and his father. A priest stands clutching a leather-bound book to his chest, his white robes pristine. He is a beacon of light against the dark rocks surrounding us. Further down the cliff is Darkwood Castle, a place I would never set foot in if my plan went off without a hitch.

The duke and his son survey me. I meet their stares with nothing but contempt in my eyes. He was there that night, Earl Bram. The hilt of his dagger protruding from my lover's back. The same ornate handle hangs from his hip now. Had he used it to cleave his head from his shoulders as well? Or was the sword dangling from his other hip the culprit of that particular crime?

I want to vomit at the sight of him, but my empty stomach will not allow it. In this moment, my decision is made. I will take him with me over the edge. My ending and my vengeance for him culminate in one rash act of defiance.

The duke looks me over with displeasure while Bram merely looks bored. It fits with his reputation. Even if I had wanted to marry him, our union would be dreadful. His reputation as a blackguard was well known. His loyalty to me would wane within a fortnight, if not the moment after his martial duties were completed. Earl Bram has a short attention span; he likes his pleasure immediate and varied.

I would've shared him with countless mistresses. In a way, I guess I'm saving us both from that sinful fate.

Bram, with his dark hair and crystal blue eyes, is handsome. He was long of leg and strong of limb—yet not even a pretty face could hide the monster he truly was. Only someone capable of true evil would've done what he did. The glint in his eye is the only hint at his true nature. I see him for what he is, and that slows my steps along the path.

My father growls low in his throat, jerking me forward.

"Behave," he snaps. "If only you had done as you were told. This would've all gone a lot smoother."

His words set my teeth on edge. After weeks of feeling nothing, I welcome the anger and let it loosen my tongue.

"I won't be your problem soon," I spit.

It is the first time I've spoken in weeks. My father hides his shock well. Even I am surprised by the feral nature of my voice. I don't have to turn around to know that my mother has turned even paler.

"Once this is done. It's done."

My father rears back, opens his mouth to speak before thinking better of whatever retort he was about to give. His head dips in a sharp nod as he pulls me more forcefully to the figures awaiting us.

A simple altar is erected at the beginning of the jagged cliff. The duke and his son stand at one side of the priest. Darkwood Castle looms far behind them, haunting this already macabre wedding scene. Below us, the waves continue to crash, echoing with the force of a thousand claps of thunder. Try as I might, I can't stop myself from glancing over to the left.

The *Whispering Woods* conceal anything inside them. The

thick treeline is dark; no light penetrates through the dense foliage. Even still, I catch whispers on the wind rising over the waves. The voices are soft and disjointed. Begging me closer and warning me to keep out all at once.

A shiver runs through me as I ignore their urgings. I will not set foot in that place again. The last time I was there, I saw him. My father had wanted me to know what had become of him.

The memory of it makes me sick, but I cannot stop myself from recalling the vision of him. How broken his body had been. My father had placed his head beside his neck as a courtesy to me, but I saw it for what it was—the death of all my hopes and dreams. My future was killed that night.

His eyes were open and milky. Their shining green irises were dim. Dirt covered his exposed skin and clung to his clothes. There was no color on his freckled cheeks. His calloused hands were cold to the touch. I had fallen atop his unmoving chest and sobbed until I was sick. My father had loomed above me, disgusted by my display over someone he deemed not worthy of it. For he may not have killed him, but he didn't stop it either.

"If only you had done what you were told. This would've all been a lot simpler."

Our steps slow in front of the altar. The duke's eyes appraise each of us individually. Earl Bram's lips tilt down.

"She looks paler than before."

The earl's frank condemnation adds another nail to his coffin.

My father chuckles heartily, urging me forward with a harsh push.

"We've just been keeping her inside. Didn't want any accidents before the big day."

The duke's dark eyes narrow.

"And have there been? Accidents?"

My father's laughter ceases, his eyes narrowing in return.

"Nothing that a firm hand and watchful eye won't prevent."

Duke Marc of Greenbrooke considers my father's words for a moment. He runs a long, fingered hand along his short white beard. He is dressed in silver and gold with not a hair out of place. He is older than my father but hardly looks it. After a tense moment, the duke nods sharply.

"We will keep an eye on her until a son is born—perhaps even two. Then we will have no need for her or her melancholic state. In the meantime," the duke pauses, nodding to his nearby guards stationed behind them.

Two men grunt as they lift a heavy chest and drag it over to my father. The hinges squeal as the lid opens, and the sight of unimaginable wealth greets my eyes. There must be thousands of gold coins in there. Jewels of all sizes and colors glow from within. My father is practically salivating over the riches.

At the top lies a piece of parchment sealed with the house crest of Greenbrooke. My father's smile widens as he reads it over, beady eyes lifting to the duke's for confirmation. The other man inclines his head.

"Congratulations on your new title and lands, Richard. She better be worth all of this."

If he weren't so wretched, I'd almost feel bad that this union won't last until the wedding feast. I will have my revenge on Earl Bram, and my only regret is that I couldn't ensure my father's demise as well.

His lands and title will die with him. That is my only solace.

The two guards heft the chest onto my parents' carriage. With one final nod, my father collects my mother by the arm and turns them both away. I try to catch my mother's eye, but it is no use. If there was any remorse in her gaze, she's hidden it well.

"You aren't staying for the vows?" Duke Marc calls out as my mother steps into the carriage.

My father laughs, then shakes his head.

"I have what I came for. She's your problem now." His eyes harden on me one last time. "Do with her as you please."

Without another word, my father glides inside the carriage, and it pulls away. The train of my wedding dress blows behind me in the salty breeze. Briny air coats my skin, causing goosebumps to break out. This is it then. I'll never see my parents again.

In the end, at least my father was truthful. A problem is all I was to them. I was not a boy who could inherit the lands. I was a girl—headstrong and wily, who had ruined herself with someone far below her station. It did not matter if I loved him. It did not matter that I would not take one coin of my father's wealth if only he had given me the freedom to be with my love.

My only value was in this betrothal. I am the only noble bride for miles. If the duke and his son had any hope for legitimate heirs, they needed to secure my hand. No matter if it was given without my consent.

Any outside force that could've prevented it from going through had to be done away with decisively and swiftly. My father saw to that. Whatever pain he caused me didn't matter because, in the end, he got exactly what he wanted. What became of me never mattered, so long as his wealth and lands grew.

"Come now, child." Duke Marc's voice rises above the sea. "Let's get this done."

At twenty-five, I am hardly a child. Any older and the duke never would've agreed to the match. It's why it all came about so swiftly. The window of time for me to make a suitable bride was rapidly closing. No matter that my bridegroom was nearly thirty, women seemed to have an expiration date men never have to contend with.

There was a time when I thought the longer I remained unmarried, the more I had a chance of choosing who I would end up with. I thought my father had learned of my desire and would be sympathetic to my plight. I had made a plan to ensure he could secure his legacy. I was a fool to believe there was a chance for even a moment.

My father had been waiting for the most advantageous proposal. The duke offered him something my rudimentary plans never could. My pleas and words of devotion were met with disdain and dismissal. It mattered little to him if my marriage was loveless—it mattered little to him if I even drew breath.

Earl Bram takes my arm.

Even with his gloves on and my sleeves, I can still feel the coldness of his palm. It radiates from the wretched heart beating inside his breast. It isn't fair that he draws breath—someone capable of such evil lives amongst us while my love rots below the ground. I must not give in to those thoughts.

The end is near. As the priest launches into his sermon, I resign myself to being patient. We aren't far from the cliff's edge. The guards are too far away to grab me. Even if I am not able to take Bram over with me, I will still greet my end with a smile. In death, I will be reunited with the one I love the most.

The rocky shore calls to me like a siren's song. Lulling me into a numb state as the priest recites the marriage vows. My own words of devotion and obedience are stuffed into the bodice of my gown. I will never say those words to Bram.

Bram's grip on me tightens as if he can read my thoughts. He stares down at me, but my gaze remains transfixed on the cliff's edge. My desire could not be more apparent. He will eventually loosen his hold. Something will distract him, and that's when I will seize my moment to finally be free.

"Do you, Earl Bram of Greenbrooke, take Lady Scarlett Crest as your one and true lawful wife?"

The priest's words shock me out of my daze. Bram's hand tightens on my arm like a vise. I have no choice but to look up at him. Were his eyes the last my love saw? Rage kindles in me, and my teeth bare of their own accord.

"I do."

Those two words echo along the barren cliff. The priest turns to me, eyes wary but expectant.

"And do you, Lady Scarlett Crest of Broken Cliff, take Earl Bram as your one and true lawful husband?"

The question is simple enough, but the reality of the vow looms. It would be easy to say the words. To lie to the priest and my would-be husband just to make it through the ceremony. Now, as the question hangs in the air, I can't get myself to say it. I cannot make a vow, even a hollow one, when I've already given myself to another. I will not ruin our sacred union with a lie.

"Say it, you petulant girl. Say it," the duke urges, jaw tight.

My heart and soul died in the *Whispering Woods*. I will not give them to another, not even as a platitude.

"Say it and let this be done," Earl Bram snaps.

His gloved hand dances along the hilt of his dagger. How I wish he'd sink his blade into me and end this all. Fire burns in his gaze, and his father curses behind me. He takes a commanding step forward as if to intimidate me into supplication.

Before he can speak, a harsh sound comes from the edge of the forest. It echoes from deep within the darkness. The sound is distinct—familiar. It draws everyone gathered for the wedding's attention. The guards turn towards it, and Bram's hand on my arm loosens a fraction. With a whistle, the duke urges his guards to inspect it.

This is my chance to make a break for it. I twist slightly, and the duke growls.

"Don't even think about trying to flee. You won't like what happens if you do," he vows.

I open my mouth, poised to retort something back and pull myself free when a gurgling sound erupts behind me. From the dense forest, the duke's guards come sprinting out. Crimson stains the front of their ivory armor as they clutch their throats. Blood seeps from between their fingers until they fall to their knees before us.

They lay there unmoving as horror settles in around us. Earl Bram screams, dropping my arm entirely and grappling for his sword. Now is my chance, time to take it.

Briny wind lacerates the exposed skin of my cheeks. The duke unsheathes his sword and stands before us, eyes trained on the forest—my stomach knots. Something tells me to wait before I take off. Armed, they could still give chase, and I have no intention of finding out what the duke plans for my punishment should I attempt to flee.

Something shifts in the treeline. If it is a person, I can hardly make out the figure. A shadow slips between the thick tree trunks, gliding between the branches like a ghost. My eyes narrow, but try as I might, I can't make anything out.

A low whistling sound whizzes through the air. Something breezes by my head, the air tousling my unbound hair. Silence comes next, only then to be interrupted by a thud. The duke's body hits the ground beside me. Blood sprays from the dagger embedded in his throat. He gasps as he tries to pull it out. The front of his fine coat is soaked in an instant. He wheezes for air, clutching at his neck until he goes still. The light in his eyes fades.

I don't have an ounce of pity for him.

Especially not as there is more movement from deep within the *Whispering Woods*. The figure, just out of sight, approaches slowly. The gruesome sight of him stills the air in my lungs.

Bram stumbles a few steps back, the sword in his hand lowering as the imposing figure comes into view.

"No," he whispers. "It can't be. It's not possible."

It isn't yet, but there is no denying what is before us.

Atop a massive black horse, a lone rider sits. Dressed in all black, his polished silver buttons glint in the light. He is tall with an enormous chest that rises and falls. Large hands grip the leather reins as he pulls the magnificent beast forward. He looks human—that is, save for the flaming pumpkin atop his shoulders.

Bright green fire spills from the eyes and mouth holes. It licks along the orange sides of the gourd. I can't believe what I'm seeing. The creature seems to be able to emote. There is satisfaction dancing in the flames of his eyes. Determination kindles the glowing green inferno within him.

As if reading my thoughts, the pumpkin's mouth spreads into a wide grin. Impossible, and yet here he is.

The priest has the good sense to scream and turn tail. Earl Bram is hot on his heels as they scramble down the narrow cliff towards Darkwood Castle. Soon their bodies are dots on the horizon. No consideration was spared for his future wife. Of course not.

Taking a deep breath, my eyes remain locked on the creature. He prowls towards me atop his massive steed. The horse scents the air before kicking at the damp grass. I have heard stories of him, as all children have. Legend says he haunts the woods, seeking revenge on the ones who stole his head. I thought it was nonsense, a way to keep curious children out of the forest after sunset. Now, I realize it was no myth at all.

For the Headless Horseman of Broken Cliff stands before me in the flesh. This is no hallucination, this is real.

The horse's eyes blaze burning red as it continues its slow approach. I don't know why I haven't run. Maybe it's because I don't have any need for self-preservation anymore. I want to die—I have for the last month since I found him. If this creature is offering me that, then I welcome him and my swift end.

The creature jumps from the horse's back. His heavy footsteps drag along the grass until he kneels down next to the duke. With a tug, he rips the dagger from the duke's throat and clutches it in his leather-glove-covered hands.

Crimson blood sparkles along the deadly, sharp blade. I can only pray it finds itself embedded in my neck next.

"Do you know who I am?"

The creature's voice rasps against my ear. Familiar and yet I know I've never heard it before. Surely I would recall meeting the Headless Horseman of Broken Cliff. The fire in his eyes slips between the holes, snapping towards me. I can feel the heat even at a distance.

I should take my chances and run. Try and fling myself from the cliff, and if his knife stops me before I can make it, then so be it. I'll have gotten what I wanted either way.

So why am I not moving?

The numbness inside me is fading. The adrenaline of all that I've just witnessed is tearing down my walls of despair.

"Do you know who I am?" the creature repeats.

I nod. Instead of fleeing, I am answering its questions. What has happened to me? A chance like this may not present itself again, yet for some reason, I don't take it. I don't want to live—and yet when faced with the certainty of death, I waver. I don't know what to make of this revelation. All of this is too confusing to bear.

The creature chuckles. With slow steps, he approaches me with the extended blade, only stopping when the sharp tip presses against the thick material of my bodice. My heart pounds wildly mere inches from the dagger's deadly edge.

Do it, I will the creature. *End me. Make the decision for me and reunite me with him.*

The creature stares at me, green flames quieting inside the pumpkin.

"No, you don't," he sighs.

The blade retracts from my chest. I refuse to believe it's relief I feel as he stows the blade.

"But you will."

Before I can say a word or make a run for it, he waves his hand. The scent of metal stings my nose and suffocates my lungs. Then there is nothing but darkness.

4

―――

THE HEADLESS HORSEMAN

She doesn't look right.

When he had lifted her into his arms and loaded her onto his horse, she had barely weighed anything. Her shockingly frail body had set his nerves on edge. Draped over his horse, he can see her with striking clarity. Something is off.

Her once luminous skin is sallow. With cheekbones sharp enough to cut himself on and hair that hangs in limp tangles down her back, something creeps into his blood. It threatens his resolve, urges him to reconsider when he would be a fool to do so.

His fingers burn with the urge to thread them through her hair. To brush them over the familiar planes of her face, but that would be unwise. He cannot be distracted by her. He's come so far, and his revenge is already in motion.

There is no space to feel anything for her beyond hatred. He will keep her with him for a time—but only as a means to an end. Only to prolong her suffering until her confession spills from her traitorous lips. He will only be granted peace once they all fall in penance for their crimes.

The demands of his creation could not have been clearer. He was forged from rage—from a soul not at rest. In this form, he would inflict his revenge. If he wanted to find peace, those responsible would be made to pay for their deeds.

A legend he was not, but one he would surely become.

Soon, blood would coat the walls of Crow Claw's Manor and Blackwood Castle. The duke died too quickly, but there was nothing to be done for it now. The others would just have to suffer more in his stead. Once they had paid the price, he would sink his dagger into her and end this once and for all.

Her betrayal was worse than theirs, and therefore her punishment had to be greater. It was what she deserved—all of it had been a lie. He died over a lie. She would know pain and fear the way he had. She would wallow in it until he granted her the mercy of death.

There is no room inside of him for kindness. His plan was already in motion. Resolve settles into his bones as he flicks the reins and urges his horse to go faster. The *Whispering Woods* rush around them in a blur as he takes her deep into the forest.

No one will find them. From this moment on, Lady Scarlett Crest is no more.

5

———

SCARLETT

Darkness greets my eyes once I'm able to blink them open.

Pain radiates from my body, but that isn't new. Feeling down myself, I find my dress intact, save for the dirt and grass stains along the tattered hem. The tight lacing is no doubt to blame for the bruising of my ribs. Each breath is shallow.

Not to mention, it's been hours since my mother's servants force-fed me one of those vile concoctions. Hunger pains shred my stomach, and I nearly double over. The pain is the only sign that I am alive, despite what I had intended for today.

The Headless Horseman had not ended me in the same manner as the duke. Instead, he brought me here—wherever I am. There is no sign of him anywhere. There aren't any signs of life in this barren room.

Beneath me was a thin, moth-bitten mattress that had seen better days. The room is devoid of furniture. The wallpaper is discolored and rolled up along the corners. The wooden floorboards are bent and eaten through. A smattering of cracked statues and dented busts linger around the room. Each one is covered in dust and thick cobwebs.

The portraits on the wall are in the worst condition. The glass is caked with grime, making it impossible to see what is depicted. A chill blows in the room, making my teeth chatter— the only light in the room comes from the open window across the way. The large pale moon shines through the room, blanketing everything in pale blue light.

My eyes snag on the open window. All is not lost yet, it seemed.

Rising on unsteady legs, I stumble over to the opening. Peering down, all my eyes can make out are the gnarled branches and thick tops of the trees below. I am only a few stories up, but that still should've been enough. If I land on my neck, death will be instant. At the very least, I'll only spend a few hours in agony before succumbing to my injuries.

Less clean than a rocky cliff, but I could make do.

Gripping the side of the window, I test the sill with my foot. The old metal groans but holds firm as I step up on it. I look down into the inviting darkness. It would take nothing to let my body fall forward and let my weight drag me down. This is what I've been waiting for. I had been so certain of today's outcome, and I could still do it. The place would be different, but the result would be just the same.

The scent of pine is heavy in the air. The cold wind burns at my eyes and cuts through my gown. My hair whips around me. I must act now before my captor returns and stops me. I lean forward into the rushing wind. A powerful gust blows me back.

A moment of panic sets in as my hand slips from the side of the window. I scream as my footing slips and the sill crumbles. Rocks fall down below as I hold tight to the frame. My breath is ragged as I fall against it.

That was my chance to be free, and yet I couldn't take it. Something stopped me—an emotion I haven't felt in a long time.

I'm scared—so scared. I haven't been able to admit it to

myself. I was a shell of a person for so long that I wished for my end to come. Now I realize that I'm as scared as ever. Frightened to live, fearful to die. I was certain for so many years of my life, and now I don't seem to know anything. Least of all what I want. Potent fear pumps through my veins. I can't go through with this—I thought I could, but I was wrong.

The truth burns me alive.

I fall back inside the room. Kneeling before the open window and cowering underneath the glowing moon, my eyes burn.

A loud bang rings out behind me, and I jump. Whirling around, the Headless Horseman looms in the doorway. His green fire burns intensely as he prowls towards me. My hands begin to tremble. Now that I have admitted I'm scared, it seems fear is the only thing I can feel. I cower under his gaze, pushing farther back against the window.

His face twists into a sneer as he glances between me and the opening.

"Were you thinking of jumping?" he demands.

Shame makes me hold my tongue and avert his gaze. There is madness in his voice. He shakes his head, flames caress his shoulders.

"Death would not spare you from me." His eyes harden. "But just to be sure."

Lifting a gloved hand, he grips the stem at the top of his pumpkin head and rips it from his shoulders. I scream at the gruesome sight. Flames remain within the gourd, and his headless body moves with ease. Without a word, he snatches me from the ground.

His arms wrap around me like iron bars, and he pulls me off my feet. We turn, and his long strides eat up the distance to the door. His head rolls after us, the flames propelling it forward.

For the first time, I itch to fight. Adrenaline pumps through me, and I thrash against his body. It is of no use, but it feels good to move, to lash out. His body never falters as I writhe in his grip—the pumpkin rolls after us with an unreadable expression.

"It was unwise to put you in that room," he admits. "I know a place where you can't do too much damage. Least of all to yourself."

I screech and buck against him. His pace picks up as we walk through the bowels of whatever castle he's keeping me in. It looks old and entirely forgotten by the world. The walls are crumbling, and the carpet is covered in leaves and dirt. Anything with value has been pilfered from here years ago.

He continues our journey until we reach a solid wood door. It swings open of its own accord and illuminates a staircase. The smell of dank and rot invades my lungs. The pumpkin head rolls after us, taking each step with ease.

"I found this place some time ago. No one will come searching for you here." His flames intensify. "You will be completely at my mercy."

I don't correct him and say, "No one is looking for me."

My father will not send a search party, nor will Earl Bram. He will inherit his father's title and say a creature stole me— that I am surely lost forever. If the Headless Horseman has taken me for ransom, he is sorely mistaken.

His feet pause on the old wooden steps. They groan under our weight, and I'm not sure they'll hold. The pumpkin head rolls back slightly to look up at me. His face is unreadable, though for a pumpkin, that's not surprising.

"Why have you not begged for your life? Pleaded to be reunited with your earl?"

I nearly laugh at his words, but somehow manage to swallow it down. I say nothing as I stare at the green flames. The fight in me dissipates as I sag against his hard body. The pumpkin sighs before rolling on, and we follow after him. The damp smell only gets worse the farther down we go.

It doesn't take me long to realize where we are. A torch illuminates outside one of the dungeon cells. The iron bars are slick with damp and grime. Without hesitation, he tosses me into the cold stone cell. The bars seal me in with a heavy clank. I don't rush towards them; there's no point.

Sludge covers my white dress in streaks of gray and black. The stone floor will bruise me before the night is up.

"You will stay in here until I have use for you," he declares.

The truth of that statement settles into my bones. I'm at his mercy. If I were unable to take my life on my terms, he would surely decide for me. He can be decisive where I am weak.

Bending down, he plucks his head up by the stem and fashions it to his shoulders again. With a wave of his hand, a metal plate appears with a small loaf of bread and a cup of water. At least he doesn't have any plans to starve me to death, it would seem.

Pity, seeing as I'm already halfway there.

Still, my disloyal stomach growls. I dare not touch it, though. Without another word, he turns and heads back towards the stairs. His figure becomes harder and harder to see as he moves away from the torch.

"What do you want from me?" I ask, shocking both of us.

His steps pause, but he doesn't turn around. I think he'll ignore my question as the silence stretches.

"Once you learn that, all of this will make sense."

Without another word, his steps echo up the wooden stairs. The sound of the heavy wooden door slamming shut makes my teeth clench. It is cold in this cell—damp. I can hear the squeaks and soft scurrying of the creatures who have been living in this castle long before I arrived.

Hopelessness presses down on me. Maybe I would've been better off jumping than being stuck here. Fear has controlled so much of my life. It was fear preventing me from leaving with *him* when I should've—it is fear that's put me in this cage. When will I ever learn?

Surely death would've been better than this. Rotting in some filthy cell all alone. I stare at the food but can't bring myself to take it. There seems to be only one thing I can do, shocking as I find it.

I pull my knees to my chest and wrap my arms around them. Then, for the first time in weeks, I do the impossible.

Cry.

6

THE HEADLESS HORSEMAN

R ib-breaking sobs echo throughout the abandoned castle.

It stirs a strange feeling inside of him. A sensation he was sure had turned to ash in the face of his molten rage. His chest aches both with this unwelcome sensation and from his efforts to ignore it.

In his heart, he longs to go to her and offer the one thing he knows she needs: comfort.

When he had come upon her in that room, had she really intended to jump? Even as his prisoner, the girl he knew never would've sought such an end. It made no sense to him. Why would she seek her death when she had not spent this last month writhing in torment as he had?

His suffering was her fault. How dare she seek to end herself before having atoned for it? He never really knew her at all. That is what he must remind himself of. No matter how much of it was real for him, sometime during those years, she became a liar. Perhaps she was one since the beginning, and liked how far she could get him to stray to please her. He had paid the ultimate price for her in the end, and she saw him put down like any other animal.

The pain comes roaring back, fresh and unyielding.

It nearly brings him to his knees as he remembers the agony of the earl's blade and his broken limbs. More than anything, he remembers her words. They were the last things he read before the final blow was delivered. He still had that physical reminder in his pocket now, and it strengthened him.

The Headless Horseman would not go to her. Not now and not ever. She could cry herself ill for all he cared—sob until her nose bled and her eyes burned. She deserved every moment of pain and fear.

It was she who kindled this rage in him. Their betrayal had been one thing, but hers—it had twisted his soul in the end. She was the reason he became this vile creature. Vengeance would be the only absolution afforded him. Her words had put him on the path to ruin.

In the end, it was her words that had echoed in his mind as the sword was raised, and it severed the head from his shoulders.

7

———

SCARLETT

There is no concept of time in this dank, dark dungeon.

Through my swollen eyes, I surmise that it must be the next day. My sobs had exhausted me enough to doze for a handful of minutes at a time. A chill damp spreads throughout my stone cell. The uneven floor bit into my bottom, and the hard wall scraped along my back.

Ripping off another piece of stale bread, I throw it into the dark side of the cell and hear the scurry of tiny feet. Best the rats keep over there and far away from me.

I finger the worn hem of my wedding dress. I had torn the large train off during the night to cover myself. The gauzy material wasn't the best at keeping out the cold, but it was better than nothing. I shivered beneath the once-brilliant fabric now gray with dirt and dust.

If the Headless Horseman never returns, I will surely perish down here. Maybe that is what he wants for me—to wallow until I meet my end, for the rats to get to me and die by a thousand tiny bites. I could make peace with that.

Dying at the hands of someone else's torment would surely

reunite my soul with his. Our ends would be similar in that way. If I were to take my own life, I could not be certain of our reunion. Would I have been damned for seeking my end? Would I be bound to that infernal manor home with my soul never knowing peace?

The Headless Horseman seeks my death. That much I know for sure.

Whatever torment he wishes to subject me to, I will withstand—fight against—until the inevitable happens. I've been living in hell for so long, I hardly know where to rank my current discomfort at being trapped here.

I wish he were with me.

It is unwise to think of him—the memories only intensify my agony, but I cannot help myself. Here in the quiet dark, there is only me and the rats. Had I not been a fool that night and run away with him as he suggested, we would be together.

Our breathing had been heavy after our lovemaking, and the promises of a tangible future were on our lips. Green and blue eyes wide with hope as we vowed never to be separated and to bide our time. It was doomed from the start, no matter how hard I tried to craft a suitable fate for us both.

I, of all people, should know nothing in this world comes for free. Good, honest people always suffer at the hands of greedy men. And *he* was the best man I ever knew. There were dozens of opportunities for the two of us to flee. If I had left with him at eighteen, the night of both of our first times, we would have a family by now.

Instead, I made us sneak around. Arrogantly thinking that we could have it all. If only I were perfect and remained obedient to my father, he would reward both of us. He had no male heirs of his own. It would take nothing more than a signed piece of paper to appoint my love the heir to his earldom. Our marriage would cement it.

My love had been with our family since he was a boy.

Having been the son of our cook. She had died during the sweating sickness, and my father kept him as a babe in his employ. Even raised him under the same roof as me until he mastered the craft of a stable boy. To my father, he was a worker.

To me, he was everything—my first friend, my first kiss, and most importantly, my first and only love.

The pounding in my chest stumbles as the moth-bitten organ gives a painful squeeze. Memories flood me, each one more heartbreakingly beautiful than the last. I can still feel him atop me. His warm, smooth skin against mine. The solid weight of him holding me close. Our mingling breaths and whispered confessions during those stolen nights have more happiness than some people get in a lifetime.

Ice solidifies in my blood. A shiver wracks my body. Memories of him are all I have now. I will carry them with me in my heart until it stops beating.

The creatures around me have stopped stirring. Apprehension tickles the back of my neck. Pale light trickles down the stairs, and I wait to hear the Headless Horseman's heavy footsteps—the torch above my cell flickers.

Through my bleary eyes, I can make out a thick fog rolling down the steps. It spreads out along the floor in a dense cloud. The damp air tickles the bare skin of my calves. Something about this doesn't feel right. I fear whatever he has hidden in the mist. No doubt it is another way to torment me.

A sharp squeak breaks through the chilling silence. Rushing footsteps echo on the stairs, but they are far too light to belong to the Headless Horseman. I push back against the stone wall. The only weapon I have won't do me much good when he wields magic.

Through the thick fog, a sound echoes. It is a short word, one I've heard before. I can barely make it out over the rushing wind. The fog grows denser, completely concealing the bottom half of my body as I sit on the floor. The sound gets closer and closer until it's finally clear.

It's a name. My name.

My mouth goes dry, and goosebumps erupt over my skin. It's my name being said by the one voice I'd never thought to hear again. I would not mistake it. There is nothing about him that I would ever forget.

It can't be—I was wrong, whatever cruelty this is, I'm not sure I'll be able to withstand. My breathing is already ragged as I stare into the fog. A voice echoes from within the mist, and a broken sob leaves me. It's him. The one I'd die for if only to see him again.

There he is coming through the fog. I can see the familiar outline of his body. Long arms and legs stop just beyond my cage. I stagger forward to grip the bars of my cell.

The cold metal stings my palms as I shove myself against them to try and get as close to him as I can.

Krane. I haven't thought of his name in a long time. Now, it is all I can think of as fresh sobs leave me. Moisture trails down my cheeks and collects at the white ribbon around my throat. My skin burns as I push against the hard metal, my fingers itching to brush against him.

The fog grows thicker, obscuring my outstretched hand. Groaning echoes from the iron as it presses into my chest, but they hold firm. I strain with all my strength to slip through.

"Scarlett!" Krane calls. "Where are you? Your father said you shouldn't be out here."

My heart breaks at his words. No, this cannot be. It makes no sense, and yet nothing has for the past month. The Headless Horseman seeks to torture me, and his magic has found the perfect way to do it. I cannot look away from the sight before me, but nor do I wish to see it.

"Krane!" I scream, stretching myself against the bars. "I'm here! Krane!"

The fog devours my words. Pushing against the bars, I feel my shoulder nearly dislocate. My fingers graze the scratchy fabric of a coat. I gasp and hook my hand around the object. A familiar forearm rests against my palm as I drag him forward.

The fog dissipates just enough for me to make him out. Worn leather work boots are laced around his feet. Dark pants give way to a long dark coat with frayed edges and missing brass buttons. I pull him closer, heart pounding at the glimpse of his bare chest.

"Krane," I whisper.

Even if I try to keep my wits about me, I cannot. I long to see him more than I care about my own self-preservation.

A wet, gargling sound falls from him. Crimson slides down his chest, making a mess of his white undershirt. The sticky red blood coats my hand, and I scream. The fog pulls back, revealing him with gruesome clarity. Blood pours from his neck as he chokes, grasping at the wound.

His beautiful face is a mess of red and black bruises. With bloodshot green eyes, he pins me where I stand. Choking and thrashing until finally his head falls from his shoulders. The body that loved me—that I knew better than my own—collapses into a heap. The hands that held me with tenderness fall to his side.

Krane's face, where I mapped the freckles on his cheeks like stars in a constellation, lies beside his torso. Lips that kissed me and called me his moon—vowed that our love was worth every risk—were now pale and unmoving. My heart shatters at the awful sight.

It is how I found him that day in the *Whispering Woods*. Earl Bram's dagger rests beside him in this recreation just as it did at the time.

I had gone searching for Krane the next morning, ready for us to make a plan to leave when he hadn't been in the stables. I hunted the grounds for him until my search took me into the forest. It was my father's guards who had found me, no doubt having heard the screams. They had brought my father to try to pry me from Krane's corpse. I would not be moved. Sobbing onto his still chest, my heart lay down beside his and died.

My father offered no condolences. Nor any retribution for the murder of one of his most loyal and longstanding servants. He had merely sneered at me that the Duke had learned of Krane's intent to ask for my hand. A slight to his son, as I had already been given to him.

It was Earl Bram's place to dispatch him as my honor demanded. My father's face had twisted in disgust as he told me it was best to keep just how long I'd been ruining myself with a stable boy to myself. The duke and his son were expecting an untouched bride.

There had been no funeral for him. No headstone to mark the ground and proclaim what a wonderful man he was. My father would not spare the coin for it and said the maggots could enjoy a fresh meal.

Now, as I stare down at his broken body once more, I see my father's desire in action. Krane's corpse begins to change color, fading from pale to blue to green. His strong body bloats and his skin stretches—the blood around his neck coagulates. The bones of his face pierce through the sinking flesh. Creatures burrow inside of him, eating away at his muscles and tendons. His milky eyes glaze over as worms push through. The wriggly, pale bodies of maggots devour his lips and tongue.

Bile races up my throat as I try to vomit. With an empty stomach, I only manage to throw up spit. A crow lands on his scalp and pecks at his eye, spearing it with its beak before devouring it whole. I scream at the creature and bang against the bars until they rattle. The fog thickens again. Krane's body is dragged along the floor until it disappears in the dense mist.

With a scream, I throw myself against the bars, willing them to snap. Wherever he has gone, I want to follow.

From the fog, the Headless Horseman appears. Green fire spills from his pumpkin as he approaches my cell. I strain against the bar, reaching with all my might. My muscles are near tearing with the force.

"Why?" I demand.

The Headless Horseman says nothing. His steps reach me, and he pauses. The flickering of his green flames stirs my ire with a swiftness. I scream and slam myself against the bars. The pain in my ribs intensifies.

"Why? Why? *Why!*"

I scream the question over and over, finally succumbing to my madness.

Tears burn my eyes. One falls down my cheek in a steady stream. He lifts a hand, and I hold my breath as his gloved fingers ghost over my face. There is something familiar in his touch, but I smack his hand away. After being numb for so many weeks, it feels nice to have this rampant emotion blazing inside of me.

I hold on to the anger and let it fuel me.

"This is only the beginning," he whispers.

Without another word, he turns on his leather boots and stomps away. The fog retreats in his wake. Once it peels back from my cell, a fresh loaf of bread and a cup of water are revealed. I groan and pull myself off the bars. What I just witnessed depletes me as I sink beside the plate of food.

How can this creature show me that? If this is the brand of torment he seeks to inflict on me, there is no way I'll survive it. Wrapping my arms around myself, I realize I'm still playing the part of a fool. I was kidding myself if I thought I was in hell before.

This is hell—actual hell. To see Krane like that again...how many times will I be forced to watch that gory scene? Seeing the one you love in such a state is not something I'd wish on my worst enemy. I feel just as hopeless as I did then.

The depth of cruelty inflicted on him is not one I can stomach. To know he was alone and cold, that I sent him to his death even inadvertently, is not something I can withstand. I don't know how long I will last in this cage if this is the Headless Horseman's method of torture.

One thing is certain: I will lose my sanity long before I lose my life.

8

THE HEADLESS HORSEMAN

Her reaction to the memory had been surprising.

He had expected her to beg for forgiveness when faced with her treachery. The moment she stared down at the corpse of the one she betrayed, she would understand that's why she was here. To atone for the sins she levied against him with her lies.

The Headless Horseman had not expected her to wail like that. Nor had he expected Scarlett to push herself so hard against the bars that she nearly shredded herself to get to the body. If she had recoiled at the sight, that would've been understandable. Instead, she reached towards it as if her life demanded it. Tried to follow it into the darkness.

Even he had felt her deep anguish. It had threatened his resolve. He had not lied to her; this was only the beginning. What was to come next would be much worse. He would lay her lies before her and demand answers.

Had she admitted to everything during this first viewing, he would've killed her and ended this cruel game. Even now, as he thinks it, he calls himself a liar. Ending her won't be easy, and after tonight, there is a voice nagging at him.

It urges him to reconsider his plan. What if he has been wrong about her? What if she is blameless in all of this—an innocent victim just like him? Could she have been ignorant of her father's plot?

Thinking back to that night is difficult, but he remembers it all with stark clarity. Her father had said she wished to be free of him. That he was keeping her from the advantageous marriage she hoped for. Earl Richard Crest had handed him the letter as proof, and indeed, that is what her words entailed.

At the time, it had seemed out of character for her, but there was no mistaking her penmanship. After all, he had received dozens of her love letters over the years. Her script was as familiar as his own.

That infernal note burned in his pocket. He should reread it. Memorize her words again so there is no wavering on what he has to do. It will burn away whatever misplaced sympathy he is feeling towards her.

She just needs to be pushed harder—tormented further. Then she will buckle and admit to her hand in the plot. He will have her confession before he takes her life. He vows this to himself. The only contrition she feels is guilt-based. She is just as responsible as the rest of them.

She has to be.

9

————

SCARLETT

The fog comes again the next night.

More forbidding mist encases me. I don't know what to expect. I want to close my eyes and curl in on myself, but I cannot seem to look away. I try to pull myself from the floor. The days spent in this cell are taking a toll on my body.

My muscles are stiff like the stone floor I've been resting on. Blood flows thickly to my limbs from lack of movement. I do nothing but recline against the hard wall and wait for another short bout of sleep to take me. Now, as the fog curls over the metal bars of my cell, I wait with bated breath. My heart pounds in my chest. If there is even the slightest chance of seeing Krane again—no matter the form—I will not miss a second of it.

I had given in and eaten some of the bread throughout the day. Though I had not wanted to, I needed to keep my wits about me. There was a reason the creature was showing me these things. To torture me, yes, but I can't shake the feeling that there is more I'm meant to understand.

Throughout my solitary day, my mind had wandered. It

didn't take me long to arrive at the idea that Krane was somehow trapped here. If this creature had his memories, perhaps he had taken his soul, possessed it, and twisted these memories to hurt me. If there was even a slight chance that my captor was hurting Krane, I had to try to free him.

If I can save him, then maybe I'll know where to meet his soul when my time comes. Maybe—

Through the fog, a figure appears, and I gasp. It is not Krane this time. It's me. Younger by nearly a decade and healthy. My long hair sparkles brilliantly even in the dark dungeon. The green dress I'm wearing molds to every curve. Pale blue eyes dance with amusement as I cast a look over my shoulder. Pink dusts both of my round cheeks.

"Come," young me urges, picking up my green skirt.

She races away in a fit of giggles before a new figure appears. A younger Krane. In the flesh, yet so far away. I crawl towards him on the stone floor. Pulling myself up, the floor cuts into the soles of my feet. I throw myself against the bars, hoping they give way. My struggle is futile.

Krane looks towards me. His verdant eyes sparkle with life. Freckles scratch along his cheeks as he laughs. Shaking his head, tendrils of reddish-brown hair cling to his ears in soft waves. The color in his face is a far cry from how he appeared the night before.

I reach out towards him, but he cannot see me. He glances up towards the ceiling in exasperation before turning towards where the younger me disappeared.

My heart aches at how handsome he is. I can hardly breathe at the sight of him alive. Dozens of memories swirl in my mind with him at the center of them all. My heart reaches for him. The frayed tendrils of my soul long to be entwined with his again.

The smell of dank blots out any trace of his familiar cinnamon and clove scent. I bought the spicy soap for him when our family would go into town. I'd smell it on my skin after I'd returned to my room after our nights together. I'd hate having to bathe the next morning, knowing his scent would be wiped from me.

This is torture to watch, but if he is trapped here by the creature, I will free him. He has already suffered enough for me. This time, I will be there to save him.

Krane pushes through the fog, giving chase to the younger me. They turn and face each other, their fronts nearly brushing.

"We need to head back. Your father will be looking for you."

Young Scarlett rolls her eyes—ever the pretty little fool.

"Stop worrying. We're almost there."

She turns and races into the fog. Krane curses and rushes after her, both their bodies disappearing into the dark. My heart lifts at the sight of us—how free we both were. It's torture to watch this knowing how it ultimately ends. If I could warn them now to keep running and never go back, I would.

We were both so young and happy. Life at Crow's Claw Manor was not dreary when he had been there. After the lessons with my tutors, I would sneak off to be with Krane. At first, it was merely to pester him while working, and then it became more. I sought him out, dragged him away from his duties, and urged him to follow me on some childish adventure. It was on one of those glorious trips that things changed between us forever.

This one, to be exact. I remember the gown well as I never wore it again.

Moments after the fog consumes them, I watch my younger self stumble in from the side. Mist curls around her heavy skirts as she wanders along in front of my cell. Off to the side is a large oak tree, in which the younger me sighs before falling against. The strong bark presses into her back. Young Krane follows over to her. There is something in his eyes that even now makes my heart race.

No one ever looked at me like that—before or since. As if I were the moon, as he called me, and his whole world orbited around me, or as if I were more marvelous than all the stars in the sky. It was apparent how much we loved each other. We were out of our minds to think we could hide it for even a moment.

Krane's steps slow as he approaches me, lounging on the tree. I stare up at him. Even at nineteen, he was taller than most grown men. Years of hard labor had outfitted him with prominent muscles.

My eighteenth birthday had come the week before. In secret, he had given me a small bouquet of wildflowers—a small gesture but one that gave me the confidence to take this next step with him.

Bracing a large hand on the bark above my head, I take in our height difference. In my satin slippers, my head barely reaches his chin. Staring up at him, love dances in my blue irises. He sees it too. I could never keep secrets from Krane. He knew me better than anyone.

"What are you doing?"

Young Scarlett smiles at his breathy question, tilting her delicate chin in invitation.

"Waiting," she sighs.

"For what?"

Krane knew—he knew everything about me from the moment we met. His green eyes kindle with awareness as their bodies drift closer. He bends down, and I watch the younger me press up on her toes to seal their mouths together. It is both of our first kisses. Chaste and unpracticed yet totally devastating.

Young Scarlett's hands tangle in the front of his white linen shirt. With a moan, she deepens the kiss and pulls him more firmly against her. His hands fall to her head, spearing into the long tendrils of her hair. My hand drifts to my lips as if I can feel his phantom kiss still. His was the only mouth I ever learned.

The only one I ever needed.

With a groan, they break apart. Both of their chests rise and fall rapidly as they stare up at each other. Young me licks over her bottom lip, wickedness in her pale blue gaze. She doesn't remove her hands, nor do Krane's slip from her head.

"Finally. I thought I would die before you ever grew brave enough to kiss me."

Krane throws his head back and laughs. The strong column of his throat catches both mine and young Scarlett's eye.

"Always one with a flair for the dramatics."

The younger me stares up at him, and I can see the decision being made. The sureness of her choice settles into her bones before my very eyes.

"You will be my husband one day."

Her declaration shatters my cold heart. Krane's lips twist into an indulgent grin.

"Will I?"

Young me nods, curling her fingers into his shirt. Krane's smile turns sad as he skims a finger along her cheek. The tenderness of his touch makes both of us shiver.

"Your father will never allow such a thing."

Pale blonde hair dances around her shoulders as she shakes her head.

"We just have to be patient. Father raised you since you were a young boy—practically as his son. If you marry me, you can become my father's heir."

Krane looks unsure, but she kisses him again, and that hesitation melts into desire.

"Trust me," young Scarlett sighs. "Everything will be alright."

The two of them don't speak of it again after that. I know

what's coming next. A sob leaves me as I watch the two of them. This is the beginning of our story—Krane and mine. It's bittersweet to watch. If given the chance, would I stop them? Knowing how our story ends, if I could warn the two of them apart, would I?

I scoff at myself. Even knowing what I know now, nothing would've kept me from Krane. He would've followed me anywhere, and I would've done the same. We are two halves of the same whole. After tonight, we were never apart again.

My heart squeezes in my chest as I watch the scene unfold. We kiss again, more urgently this time. Tasting and testing each other's tongues with deliberate strokes. Together in a mess of brushing fingers and jumbling thumbs, we shed each other's clothing. Krane stares at me in wonder—the only man to have ever seen my naked flesh. He lies me down atop my discarded gown.

This first time was all about exploration. In the coming years, he would learn everything about my body. How to make me combust with only a few twists of his fingers inside of me. Still, as unpracticed as it is, there is something so beautiful about the two of us. Finding solace in each other's embrace for the first time.

There is pain, but one that is relieved by Krane's firm kiss. He pulls back just slightly to take in our two bodies as they connect. Young Scarlett's hand drifts to his left shoulder and traces the birthmark there. The pale mark is heart-shaped. She presses a kiss to it before falling back to the ground.

When they are done, they hold each other close. Their sweaty brows press together. Soft kisses are bestowed. Krane stares down at her with a fierceness that never leaves his gaze again.

"I love you, Scarlett." His voice is still rough from their lovemaking. "I have from the first moment I saw you. My heart is yours."

Tears dance in her blue eyes, and she holds him closer.

"I love you, too. Nothing will ever keep us apart."

Fog envelopes the delicate scene before me. It wraps mist around them like two strong arms and pulls them away. I sag against the bars of my cell, the strength in my body leaving me. That beautiful scene was a different type of devastating. The sight of Krane's corpse was one thing—shocking, abhorrent.

This, however, was more painful. To see how happy we were, to know there was a chance for us to escape. We should've gotten back into our clothes and left Broken Cliff never to return. We would've been destitute, but we would've had each other. That was all that mattered after all.

My heart aches for the two young people who had their future ahead of them. If someone had asked me back then if I thought this current hell I was in was possible, I would've laughed in their face. My father could never be considered charitable, but to wed me to a monster like Bram, who so sense-lessly killed Krane, was unthinkable. There was a time I believed my father had loved Krane as a son.

All of that was lost to his greed. Now we were all suffering because of it.

Through the fog, heavy footsteps glide closer. The mist pulls back to reveal the Headless Horseman's imposing form—his silver buttons gleam in the dim light of the dungeon. Green fire snaps from between the pumpkin's holes. His mouth twists in disdain.

"Foolish children," he growls.

The warmth of that sacred memory ices over. A coldness settles along my bones as I stare up at the Headless Horseman. I bare my teeth at his callous words.

"If he had not been a love-struck fool and trusted your word, he would still be alive."

A punch to the stomach would've hurt less than his words. I

double over as if he struck me, nonetheless. His condemnation sets me on edge.

"You're the reason he's dead."

My eyes widen, and I grip the metal bars in my palms. They groan as I squeeze them. My anger flares to life within me. This unbridled rage settles a fine red mist over my vision. All the poison on my tongue aims at the creature across from me.

"How dare you say that. You have no idea what you're talking about," I snap.

The Headless Horseman laughs as green flames fall from his mouth.

"I know everything. I was there that night."

His words steal my breath. He was there? That's not possible. Is it? Unease curdles my stomach, and my former theory of Krane being the Headless Horseman's prisoner seems to be affirmed. He must have trapped Krane's soul somehow and is now using it to torment me. How else would he get these memories? That is the only explanation I can think of.

The thought of Krane still suffering insenses me. I bang against the bars.

"What have you done to him?" I demand. "Let me go this instant!"

The Headless Horseman shakes his head, creeping closer to where I remain locked up. Righteous anger burns me alive. I hate this creature.

"What will you do? Kill me?" he asks.

"If I must. If you are keeping Krane somewhere—"

The Headless Horseman roars. The rocks around me shake from the force of his anger. Tiny pebbles and dust fall onto my shoulders from the ceiling. His large hands grip the metal bars. His large pumpkin pushes against them, green flames nearly singeing my skin. I meet his harsh stare with one of my own.

"Do not speak his name. You do not have the right!"

His words hit like a smack.

"If it weren't for you, he would still draw breath—you are the reason he's dead."

Those words lacerate me with the force of a thousand cuts. Cold and callous, yet they are shockingly accurate. It is my fault that Krane is dead. While I did not hold the dagger that killed him, I surely sentenced him to death.

If I had not told him about Earl Bram's proposal, he never would have propositioned my father to accept his suit instead. The earl never would've killed him for the slight. Even if he had believed the rumors about the two of us, it wouldn't have been enough to act on.

It is my fault. Why hadn't I left with him? It is a question I'll ask myself until I draw my final breath. Regret drains all my fire. I slink back into my cell, falling against the rough wall. The Headless Horseman pulls back, releasing the bars with a groan.

"Now you're beginning to see the truth."

I manage to shake my head but can't seem to meet his eye.

"If you wish to punish me, then do so. I will not fight you on that. But if you have Krane's soul, please release it." A broken sob leaves me. "He never deserved any of this."

Fresh moisture coats my cheeks as I fall to the ground. Green flames lick along the sides of the pumpkin as the Headless Horseman is quiet for a moment. I don't think he's going to answer until his whole body shifts.

"His soul is within me. It can never be freed."

My head jerks up, but only in time to watch him disappear into the dense fog. There will be no fresh bread or water tonight. The mist rolls away until there is nothing left behind. A new chill permeates my cell, and I curl in on myself. I'm more confused than ever.

The only thing I am certain of is that if Krane's soul is trapped within that creature, I must find a way to free him. That is why I could not end myself, even when the moment presented itself. I still had work to do here—a purpose. I will free Krane if it is the last thing I ever do.

Is it possible the Headless Horseman killed him? My father had claimed Earl Bram responsible, and there had been his dagger left behind, but Krane's demise was exceptionally brutal. Earl Bram had a horrible reputation, but none of it mentioned the level of violence needed for such a killing.

Confusion causes my head to pound, and I let it fall back against the cold stone wall. I should get some rest. Who knows what tomorrow will bring? I open my eyes with some effort and look towards the stale piece of bread. I should eat some to keep my strength up.

As I go to crawl over to the plate, something catches my attention.

The bars to my cell are different than before. I shakily rise onto my feet. My hands trail along the metal feeling the crushed grooves from the Headless Horseman's grasp. They have been bent and pulled apart just wide enough for me to slip through.

I've never been more grateful for my slighter frame than I am now. The fit is tight. I have to bend and twist my body at odd, painful angles, but I manage to get my shoulders through. Yanking on the bar, I pull my lower half through and stand on the other side of my cage.

I stare up into the darkened stairwell. With a deep breath, I know what I must do.

Enjoying my freedom for only a moment longer, I quickly crawl back through the opening. It is easier now that I know how to twist myself. I will only get one shot at what I've planned, and I need to make it count.

Reaching below the fluffy hem of my dress, my hand drifts to my right thigh. The Headless Horseman should've searched me before locking me in here. The small dagger sheathed there was only meant to end Earl Bram, should I not have been able to take him over the cliff with me. My father's guards were always careless with their weapons; this one was easy enough to poach.

I thought of using it against myself a dozen times, but my hand could never go through with it. Now I realize it was because I needed to live to make it here. Freeing Krane from this creature was my sole mission now. I don't care what becomes of me so long as he is at rest.

I grip the simple handle in my palm. This dagger was meant for an earl, but it will soon find itself a new victim: the Headless Horseman.

10

SCARLETT

When the fog rolls in the next night, I am ready. My decision has been made, and now I must wait for the opportunity to present itself. The moment he appears, I will surprise him. At no point did the bars straighten themselves out. I can still break free, and the Headless Horseman will pay for his mistake.

The fog deepens, and from within it rises a full moon. The glowing orb casts a blue light onto the ground below. The mist snaps and flows like waves against a rocky shore. From its depths, a new scene is revealed. Two naked bodies are tangled together atop a blanket in my father's stables.

Long pale fingers trace his heart-shaped birthmark, while his tan hands slide through silvery–blonde hair, resulting in a throaty sigh. It is Krane and I again, the age we were a month ago. *Not this night,* I think. *I don't know if I can bear watching it.*

I grip the bars in my hands, the cold metal biting into me.

"My moon." Krane smiles before taking the other me's lips in a tender kiss.

It may only be a month ago, but the difference between the two of us is shocking. I looked so alive back then. My body had filled out in the form of full breasts and round hips. My pale skin was luminous, and my hair was thick and long. A far cry from the starving wraith I was now.

"My sun." She breaks their kiss and rubs her forehead against his pink shoulder. "Seems as if you got too much of it today."

Her lips find his birthmark and place a kiss atop it. It was the last sunny day I can recall Broken Cliff having. Since Krane was killed, we have lived in darkness. The sky blighted us in punishment for killing someone so wonderful.

While the love in her eyes is real, there is a trepidation in her movements. Her smile is brittle as she stares up at him, and I know all too well what's plaguing her. My father had come to me shortly before I left to find Krane in the barn. I was a fool to think that making it to twenty-five unmarried was a good sign.

He had caught the two of us together less than a month before this. I was not ignorant of the rumors swirling around Krane and me. We were not nearly as discreet as we should've been. However, whispers and rumors were one thing, and my father discovering us with his own eyes was quite another. I had foolishly hoped that he ignored the gossip because he believed in our love. How wrong I had been.

I shouldn't have said anything, I will past me not to speak. To keep this news to herself and leave with Krane this instant.

I am powerless to do anything but watch the end of us unfold.

"Krane," past me whispers. "There is something I have to tell you."

I grip the bars, and bile swims up my throat as I watch her relay the news to him. I lived it, and yet somehow seeing it from this angle is worse. I hear her say that she is engaged to Earl Bram. My father was forcing the match, and in one month, the two of them would be married.

"No," Krane snarls. The impressive muscles of his abdomen tighten as he sits up. "That cannot be."

Past me rises beside him, gripping his arm and pleading with her eyes.

"I refused my father, Krane. Told him I would rather die than marry the earl." She laughs without humor. "He cared little for my opinion on the matter. The price they're willing to pay for me is too high."

"You cannot marry him. You are already married to me, Scarlett."

My heart trips over itself. The memory of our small ceremony comes rushing back. The two of us had snuck away into the *Whispering Woods* with a ribbon and a knife. Our palms had bled, and our fates were sealed in the old way. Our vows of forever were shared during each fevered kiss and teeth-chattering moan.

The cut on my palm was barely a scar anymore, but it had meant everything. It still does.

"Our handfasting will not sway my father. He will take it as the slight it is."

Krane drags a hand through his red hair, muscles tensing.

"Then leave with me. Now."

He grips her face in his hands. She cradles his hands, her smile turning sad.

"And go where?"

"Anywhere." Desperation laces each of his words.

"Go with him," I whisper between the bars. "Be free."

Krane presses on, my words swallowed up by the fog. I cannot change what is about to come.

"I have money. As long as we are together, it doesn't matter."

Tears fall heavily down her cheeks.

"Life would be difficult. Not to mention the duke would come after us. Probably enlist some of the king's guards to help."

Krane kisses her fiercely. I still feel the searing press of his lips. The last ones we'd ever shared. I will my past self to savor it.

"Let them come," he says. "I'd rather die than be without you."

A smile twists the lips of me from a month ago.

"Now who's the dramatic one?"

He kisses her again, nipping at her lower lip.

"Still you."

Pulling apart, she tucks a longer piece of red hair behind his ear.

"Let me think on it, okay? Give me some time to form a plan."

My voice grows hoarse as I scream at her not to go. I urge them both to get dressed, steal one of my father's horses, and never look back. They don't hear me. Not as they both rise and share a parting kiss. Brushing the hay from her hair, I love you's are shared one final time. Krane watches her as she slips from the barn and into the quiet main house.

"Go, Krane," I sob. "Leave me behind. Save yourself."

He would never do that. Krane was a good man, kind and loving. The kind of man my father could never dream of being. He was honest, and that honesty got him killed. Krane put his trust in the wrong people—me, my father. While I may not have killed him outright, my love for him caused his death— my arrogance in wanting us to have the life I always envisioned left him vulnerable.

He loved me and my father, and in the end, we both betrayed him. Krane had thought that if he approached my father, man to man, and asked for my hand, he would hear him out. Honesty and true love weren't going to fill my father's coffers, nor would they sign over new lands to him.

We were always doomed to meet this end, cursed by one man's ambition.

The memory swirls into the fog. The tendrils lick over Krane until he is gone. From its depths, a new setting emerges. I watch as Krane, dressed in his simple clothes, approaches Crow's Claw Manor in the dark. He looks both ways before opening the door, trepidation in each muscle.

Unease grips me as I watch Krane walk along the front room. He pauses outside my father's study. Voices echo deep from within. Three to be exact. My stomach sinks.

After I left Krane in the stables, I slipped in through the back of the house. I had no idea they were there that night.

The oak door to my father's study pushes open, and there they are. My father, clutching a glass of brandy beside a roaring fireplace adorned with a proud stag's head, and Duke Marc of Greenbrooke and his son Bram. All three sets of eyes turn towards Krane as he enters the room.

His simple clothes are a far cry from the gaudy embellishments emblazoned on the three men surrounding him. Krane stands out amongst them despite that. He is taller than the duke and his son, nearly a head taller than my father. He is stronger than all of them. His beauty easily eclipses that of the awful prince.

The scent of smoke and pine dances throughout the dungeon. The heat of the fire licks along my body. Krane bows to them, ever the dutiful servant. My stomach rolls at the subservience. He was always seen as beneath them when he was better than all of us.

"Krane," my father says with surprise. "What are you doing here?"

Krane's cheeks heat. It would be unusual for him to be in my father's study, especially without invitation. Not to mention the last time they were face-to-face, he had been inside of me. Still, he clears his throat and straightens his spine.

"Sir, I wanted to—"

"Offer congratulations to the duke and his son. Earl Bram and Scarlett will make their union formal in a month."

There is a glint in her father's eye I don't miss. This was his way of giving Krane an out. If he had agreed to his words and left, my father would've let him live. At least he would've let him live long enough to escape. But Krane was too headstrong—too in love to heed the subtle warning.

I see it all the same, and my stomach rolls.

Krane shakes his head, squaring his shoulders once more.

"I came to speak about that with you." He swallows loudly. "I wanted to ask you—beg you—to wed her to me instead."

There is silence for a moment. The three men look at each other before breaking into riotous laughter. My father nearly doubles over as he wipes tears from his eyes. Both the duke and his son look smug. Color floods Krane's cheeks and stains the tops of his ears.

I want to go to him and shield him from their cruelty. My heart breaks for him—how earnest his plea was and the callous laughter it was met with. I should've killed my father when I had the chance.

Krane weathers their indignation, never backing down.

"Wed her to you?" my father asks once he catches his breath. "Have you lost your mind? A poor stable boy? A bastard with no family name to speak of? What could you even possibly offer that would tempt me into giving you her hand?"

"I love her—have since we were children." Krane braves my father's cruel remarks. "We handfasted in the woods. She is already my wife."

The laughter in the room dies like a candle being blown out. Something forbidding settles amongst the party. I can feel it from where I am trapped. Ice nails of apprehension claw down my neck.

"Richard," Duke Marc hisses. "This will not do."

My father licks his lips before draining the rest of his

brandy. Whatever tenderness he felt towards Krane is gone. That glint in his eye deepens and lays bare the rotten soul he's always possessed.

"No. No, it will not."

My father walks over to Krane and claps him on the shoulder. My love is surprised but holds fast. With a sigh, my father shakes his head.

"Since you two decided to wed without my knowledge in the old way, then you will earn her hand in the same manner." He squeezes Krane's shoulder in his meaty fist. "You will have to prove yourself."

Krane looks apprehensive but takes the bait.

"How?"

"Simple. By going into the *Whispering Woods* and locating the pumpkin used by the headless rider. I'm sure you know the stories." Krane nods, and my father continues. "Bring it to me before dawn, and I will give my daughter to you. It will be a sign that the old gods have blessed your union."

"Richard—"

My father holds up a hand to silence the duke.

"It is a folk tradition. One that shouldn't be taken lightly."

"Sir, isn't the headless rider a legend? How will I—"

"If you wish to have my daughter, those are my demands that must be met."

Krane still looks unsure, but I can see the hope in his green eyes. He would do anything to have me. Even fall for my father's ruse. His betrayal is evident now. The part he played in Krane's demise is larger than I ever thought. To know he was the one who sent him into the woods—the room spins around me, and I grip the bars to keep upright.

"Go fast." My father claps Krane on the shoulder again. "We'll be waiting for you at the woods' edge at dusk."

"Thank you, sir. You won't regret this."

My father inclines his head as Krane rushes from the room.

The fog swirls around the scene, twisting it and forming a new shape. The thick rows of trees loom behind Krane, who is already caked in dirt as he looks for the fabled pumpkin my father demanded. Dirt clings to his hair and clothes.

I have to stop this—stop him. This might be my last chance to do so. I was going to wait for the Headless Horseman, but what if this is what I was meant to do instead? This may be the only chance to free Krane from the creature's grasp and let him finally have peace. If only I could save him from his fate.

"Krane," I scream, reaching through the bars.

He travels deeper into the woods as I call his name over and over again. The fog swirls to keep up with his movements. His body gets swept further away from me as tendrils of mist encase him. My hand reaches forward and feels only damp air.

Without giving myself a chance to reconsider, I slip through the opening of the bars and rush forward. I dive into the thick fog, unable to see my hand in front of my face.

"Krane!' I call. "Krane! Leave this place while you still can!"

My fingers find nothing but air as I rush deeper into the fog. I don't know how far I run for, or even how it's possible. For a moment, I think I'll be trapped in this unending fog forever. That is, until I hear the sound of thunderous hooves and two strong arms bracketing me.

"You cannot run from this," the Headless Horseman snarls in my ear.

Green flames lick over my shoulder as I thrash against him. I buck against his hold, but there is nothing that can be done.

"Before the sun rises, you will see what you have done, and you will pay for it."

The fog recedes, and the scene before me comes into view. The breath in my lungs freezes, and so do my movements. I scream. I don't want to see this, but it can't be stopped.

In this creature's arms, I am powerless. All I can do now is weep.

11

THE HEADLESS HORSEMAN

H e does not wish to watch, but he must.

The Headless Horseman holds her thrashing body close. Despite her gaunt frame, there is something comforting about having her close. A dormant part of him stirs at the sensation, and he growls at it. There is no place for tenderness here. He will not enjoy her warmth—not allow it to stir long dormant memories—all of this is a means to an end.

And her end has come at last.

After she witnesses her atrocities and confesses to her treachery, she will beg for his forgiveness. He will not give it. The only salvation he will offer her in the end is death. May her soul be tormented for eternity for what she has done.

It is only fair after all. She brought about his end, and now he will bring about hers.

Scarlett's struggling ceases as the fog around them swirls. The dense mist ripples in the dark dungeon, expanding farther than should be possible. There in the darkness, it finally recedes. From inside the fog, the red-haired man, Krane, appears.

Dirt streaks his clothing and hair as he navigates through the dark woods. He gracefully jumps over large boulders and dodges behind sturdy trees. Krane hunts for the pumpkin head. His quest is as futile as it is earnest. All of this to win his lover's hand, what a fool he had been.

Krane was so absorbed in his task that he didn't hear them approach. Not until it was too late, his fate sealed in the *Whispering Woods*. The harbingers of his death linger for a moment, watching his useless search with thin-veiled amusement.

The Headless Horseman swallows his growl. There is no use in trying to change the past. What's done is done.

Earl Richard Crest, Duke Marc of Greenbrooke, and his son Bram linger at the treeline. Krane finally realizes there is an audience behind him. Setting down a large rock, he wipes his filthy palm on the threadbare material of his pants.

"What are you doing here?" he asks. "I thought I had until dawn."

The Headless Horseman grinds his teeth together. The earnestness in the man's green eyes is unparalleled. There is no apprehension—no distrust. His kind nature had been his undoing. If only he had been wary of this family—of her—fled when he had the chance, everything would've been different. He was a fool to think himself special. No one goes against the Crest family and lives to tell about it.

Richard Crest steps forward, the other two men tight behind him, gloved hands resting on their sword hilts. Only then does Krane pause and narrow his eyes. *Run,* the horseman urges, *leave while you still can.* Krane does nothing but stare at the man he once considered a father. The patriarch of the only family he had ever known—the man he wished to call his father-in-law someday.

Scarlett's breathing picks up. Soft tendrils of her hair tickle his face. She's gone whiter than a sheet. Finally, she realizes what's about to happen and understands the sins she will have to answer for.

"I thought so, too." Richard's eyes harden. "Until I received an alarming update."

Krane's red brows pull low. The three men stand just before him. Their eyes glow like serpents ready to strike. They'll end an innocent man in pursuit of their greed. He should've known she was just like them, had only been kidding himself that she was somehow different. One cannot be raised in cruelty and expected to become a saint. Her soul is just as twisted as theirs, no matter how perfectly it fits with his own.

"My daughter was informed of your offer of marriage. When I told her of our bargain to gain her hand, she was... disturbed."

A broken sob cracks from Scarlett's lips. The Headless Horseman tries not to grin in satisfaction at her despair.

"She lamented that while she possessed some form of childhood affection towards you, it had come to an end. Whatever was once between the two of you, she wishes to be over. Her desire now, above all else, is to be united with Earl Bram."

"No," Scarlett whispers.

He gazes down at her pale face. Tears stain her cheeks. A pretty convincing performance, though now he recognizes that she was always a compelling actress. So much so that Krane is stunned at her father's words. He blinks a few times as if not registering what the other man has declared.

"You see, she wants someone who can provide her with the life she is accustomed to. Wealth and comfort—something you wouldn't understand, my boy."

Color splashes across Krane's freckled cheeks. He shakes his head, even as he stumbles back as if in a daze.

"No—no, that can't be. She loves me. She told me—"

Earl Richard digs deep into his pocket and produces a carefully folded note. The sight of it makes the Headless Horseman snarl. He extends the parchment to Krane, who takes it in his trembling hand.

"It is all right here if you don't believe me. Signed by her and everything."

A weak protest slips from Scarlett's lips. She has gone completely limp in his arms. Now that her treachery has been revealed, there is nothing left to do but succumb to her own betrayal.

Green eyes roam over the delicate parchment. Tears collect on Krane's lower lashline, but he blinks them away, not wishing to show weakness. The letter has its intended effect. From here, the Headless Horseman watches the young man's heart shatter in his chest. He can still feel the jagged edges of it puncturing through his skin.

"I still don't understand." Krane's voice is barely above a whisper.

"Women are fickle, my dear boy. Surely you recognize her handwriting. This is no trick."

And recognize her handwriting, he does. With trembling hands, Krane refolds the parchment paper, tucking it into his pocket. Why he kept it, he still doesn't know. One last keepsake from her, he supposes.

"If this is what she wants, then I will go at once."

Scarlett shudders in his arms. Glistening tears spill down her neck and soak the ribbon around her throat. She begins to shake violently. Teeth clatter with each broken sob.

Richard sighs and shakes his head.

"I'm afraid it's not that simple." The other two men come up to flank him, ready to cut Krane down. "An alarming report that you have spoiled my daughter has reached the duke and his son. If that is the case, then payment must be taken. In whatever form her intended demands."

The Headless Horseman has to scoff. There was no report. Earl Richard had caught the two of them nearly a month before. He hadn't cared for the rumors swirling about his daughter and Krane until it would somehow impede the money the duke was willing to give him.

Then retribution had to be taken.

To his credit, Earl Bram looks bored. The hand on his dagger is loosely wrapped. He merely shrugs as the other two men look towards him.

"Let the poor bastard go. I care very little about fucking a virgin on her wedding day."

Duke Marc growls at his son.

"Your flippant attitude is unbecoming." His blue eyes bore into Richard's. "We seek the stable boy's head as payment."

"No!"

Both Krane and Scarlett scream the word in tandem. The Headless Horseman ensures her eyes are open. She will bear witness to everything that comes next.

"Please, sir. I beg you. I've been with your family for years. I've been loyal, I've—"

"Hush, dear boy," Richard coos. "It will all be over soon."

Quick as lightning, Earl Richard Crest unsheathes his dagger and embeds it into Krane's abdomen with a sickening squelch. Scarlett screams in his arms, thrashing against his hold. Krane huffs in pain, clutching his stomach as Richard removes the blade now coated in crimson.

Duke Marc appears behind Krane as he staggers back. He wastes no time tripping the younger man and kicking him into the dirt. Krane groans and grunts at each sharp pounding of the duke's steel-toed boot. Once both of his green eyes begin to swell, the duke bends down and hefts him onto his feet. His deadweight is cumbersome, but somehow the duke manages.

"Do it, Bram. Sink your blade into him."

"Father, is this really ne—"

"Do it!"

Rolling his eyes, Earl Bram stalks behind the bleeding

Krane. Unsheathing his ornate dagger, he embeds it into the man's back. His screams echo throughout the woods. Birds and creatures take refuge in the surrounding trees to hide from the mutilation.

"Good," the duke purrs, releasing Krane.

He stumbles forward a step, miraculously still on his feet. Trying to open his swelling eyes is useless. Blood pours from his nose and mouth. The wound to his stomach weeps through his open hands. Krane carries the scent of death with him. He already looks more like a monster than a man.

Earl Richard unsheathes his sword—the silver metal glints in the moonlight.

"KRANE!" Scarlett screeches, trying to reach for him.

The Headless Horseman snarls at her. How dare she pretend to care now? It was her words that caused all of this. Her fictitious love sent him to his death as certain as if she stabbed him herself.

"His head, my lord."

With one mighty swing, his sword whistles through the air and cleaves Krane's head from his shoulders in one blow. His body collapses into a pile of bent limbs. Blood spurts from the gaping hole in his neck. Scarlett screams, her voice sharp as nails. Over and over she shrieks as his head rolls away. Eyes still cracked open and staring up at her.

She thrashes and bucks, but it is of no use.

They watch as her father kicks his head back over to nestle beside Krane's fallen body. The three men return to each other's sides before turning towards their horses

"She'll go looking for him tomorrow. We'll leave the body here for her to find." Earl Richard shakes his head. "This is all her doing after all."

"No," Scarlett chokes. "No, no, *no*."

"Yes," the Headless Horseman snarls.

The fog swirls around them, coating Krane's corpse in mist. The moon above changes into a golden sun before shifting back into a pale waning moon. This is it. Now she will finally understand what her betrayal has wrought.

Releasing her sobbing body, Scarlett falls to the floor with a thud. She wastes no time in rising and rushing over towards Krane. The fog wraps around both of them. Her chest shakes with the force of her cries. Throwing herself down atop him, she wails into his bloodied shirt. Gripping the fabric until her fingers turn white, she says something to him that the Headless Horseman cannot hear. More lies, he is certain.

With a wave of his hand, Krane's corpse is snatched out from underneath her. Falling onto her knees, she screams, reaching into the mist, his body disappeared into. Whipping around, fire burns in her pale blue eyes. With an unbridled scream, she reaches under her dress and unsheathes a small dagger. What damage she thinks she can inflict with that, he is not sure, but she rushes toward him with the blade extended all the same.

Her pale fingers find his coat, ripping it open to expose where his heart should be.

"Let him go! Let him go!"

The dagger looms closer to the gray skin of his chest, but he thwarts her attempts easily. Bracketing her delicate wrist, he stays the weapon in her hand. He whirls her around so that she can witness the final act of the show—the last memory he has —the one that will bring all of this together.

Inside the fog, Krane's corpse rests broken on the ground. A deep rumbling shakes the ground beneath their feet. Large cracks begin to form, spilling tendrils of glowing green fire. Krane's body slithers down into an opening, a fresh flame spitting out in his wake. Scarlett screams again, pushing against her captor.

From the broken earth, two figures emerge—one a midnight-colored steed, with glowing red eyes and sharp teeth. The next is a solitary pumpkin, large and ripe. From the flames, Krane's body is lifted by strong tendrils of fire. It holds him high as the flames consume him. They flow into his body, reknitting bone and sealing broken skin.

Their magic lengthens his limbs and strengthens his chest. Pale skin gives way to a dark gray. His severed head is given to the pumpkin. Fire encases them both until one is ash, and the pumpkin is carved with large eyes and a mouth opening. The gourd is then slammed onto his shoulders. The eyes and mouth stretch as green flames spill from within.

The creature levels a stare at her, allowing her to take in his foreboding form. Scarlett sucks in a breath, her eyes wide with disbelief. The creature mounts his steed and rides off into the fog, green flames burning away the last of the mist.

She turns in his arms. The Headless Horseman growls down into her face.

"Confess," he spits.

It has all been revealed now. The moment of his creation has unfolded. She has no choice but to own her part in all of it now. This is what befell the lover she so callously dismissed. If only she had spoken to him truthfully, he would've been alive. She had sought the coward's way out through her note. His death was on her hands for the part that she played—another plaything to a powerful family—discarded once they became bored.

The Headless Horseman expects her to deny it. She will downplay whatever role she had in the hopes of sparing herself. He wills her to come clean so that he might end this. The rage he feels pumps thickly through his veins. Her confession will seal her fate and set her free.

She never loved him. He has to hear her say it. Once he has her confession, this first part of his revenge will be complete.

The others still left will suffer too, only not as elaborately as her. They may have driven their blades into him, but she had broken his heart. The vows of eternity they swore meant nothing to her, and that is why her punishment would be greater than theirs.

They may have killed him, but what she did hurt for more than any sword could.

He had spent a month replaying the years they spent together. Each solitary moment spent in the darkness fueled his anger. Each whispered confession, every vow swam in his mind with new clarity. All of them point to the same conclusion.

She had never loved him. She had never loved him. She—

Her confession never comes. Her struggling ceases as she stares up at him, almost like she is in a dream. Tears collect in the corners of her eyes, but they do not fall.

"Krane?"

Her voice is as soft as summer rain. With trembling hands, she peels back his coat. There, etched onto his gray skin, is his pale heart-shaped birthmark. Scarlett gasps.

"Krane," she repeats. "It's you."

SCARLETT

Krane is alive.

The reality of those words shocks me to my core. He is alive, and he is the Headless Horseman. How can that be? Why has this all happened? Confusion flows through me. I am a mess of conflicting emotions, but one outweighs them all. Happiness.

Krane is *alive*—my Krane.

It all seems so obvious now. The familiarity in the Headless Horseman's touch. How part of me knew him even if I didn't know how. I can see it all now—feel it too—his familiar heartbeat pounds against my flattened palm. The soft brush of his soul against mine as we stare at each other is a feeling I know all too well.

So what if he has a pumpkin for a head? I love him just the same. I'd recognize him in any form.

"You were dead," I whisper. "I saw the body. How did you—why did you—"

My fingers dance along his birthmark. How many hours have I spent tracing the shape? Countless. I thought I'd never touch it again, and now I can't seem to stop.

The Headless Horseman—Krane—snarls at me before shoving me away. Instantly, I am freezing—the temperature of the dungeon plummets. The rage inside his eyes brings me up short. My Krane would never push me away. He would never look at me with anything less than adoration.

Everything makes sense to me now.

I understand his anger, even if it is misdirected. My father's betrayal was more complex than I could've ever imagined. He made me complicit in his foul deeds. It wasn't enough to kill Krane, but he had wanted him to suffer and think that in his final moments, I had rejected him for another. They will all pay for their hand in this.

"Krane."

I keep my voice soft, approaching him carefully like a wounded animal.

"Stop saying my name! Confess," he hisses.

Taking another tentative step towards him, I hold up my hands. My small blade is still clutched in my palm, and I quickly return it to the sheath. Trying another step, he growls and fire snaps at me from inside the pumpkin.

"None of it's true." I swallow thickly, desperation causing sweat to slide down my back. "I never went back on my word to you. I love you."

"Liar!" he snarls, lunging towards me.

I hold my ground. I can't cower in the face of his rage. If there is any chance of getting him to realize the error of his thinking, I must be unwavering.

"It's true. I've always loved you. From the moment you saved me from drowning in the pond when I was seven until right now. I have loved you and only you."

Krane pulls back, his hand curling into fists at his sides. I press on undeterred.

"Look at me," I command, gesturing towards my body. "I've been dying without you."

His angry eyes track down my body. Shaking his head, I know he can see the difference in me, even if he doesn't want to admit to it.

"What my father said to you was a lie."

"No."

He spits the word at me while digging into his worn pockets. Rummaging around, he pulls out a crumbled piece of parchment. It is stained with all manner of dirt and blood. The folders are deeply creased, as if read over and over.

"What would you make of this then?"

With a flick of his wrist, the parchment flies towards me. I catch it between my palms and fold the worn pages back. The words on the page make my stomach sour. I devour each hateful, deceitful sentence. All of it is a disavowing of our connection—that it was nothing more than a childhood fantasy that had gone too far.

It makes me sick to read, but I must admit the script is familiar. As is my signature at the bottom.

"I didn't write this. It's a forgery."

Krane laughs without humor, his eyes dimming inside the pumpkin sockets.

"Can you do anything besides lie?"

Indignation sparks within me and loosens my tongue.

"It's the truth."

I can't imagine what he's been through. The pain of dying—of thinking I abandoned him in his final moments for the sake of money and titles. His body was twisted into this infernal form, bent on getting revenge and letting that anger fuel him. My heart begins to clench in my chest.

If I cannot break through to him, I could lose him again. This time, permanently. I wish I had a way to prove the letter was fake. If only I had—

A gasp rips through me. My hands dive into the bust of my gown. Beneath the tight boning and stiff fabric, I find what I'm looking for. The parchment crunches against my fingers as I pull it from beneath my breast.

Pulling out my creased vows, I hold them beside the offending note. I hear Krane drift closer as I survey the two writings. They are remarkably similar, just as she intended them to be.

"Look," I say, holding up both notes to him. "Look at how the i's are dotted here and the swirls at the end of all the y's. Now compare them with this note."

I thrust both papers towards him, which he thankfully takes. His eyes rove over each before looking up at me. His expression is unreadable.

"What is this?"

I cringe at the question, not wanting to answer.

"My marriage vows to Bram."

Krane growls, flames snapping inside his pumpkin.

"More proof of your treachery."

"I didn't write those words," I snap, before pursing my lips. "I mean, I did—I copied them from my mother. Whose handwriting is remarkably similar to mine."

My heart sinks at the words I'm about to say next. Krane looks at me with unflinching awareness.

"Don't you see? It was she who wrote this note my father gave to you."

The depth of her betrayal hurts me. My father's treachery was well known, but to think that she could also be complicit shocks me even now.

"I didn't even know the duke and his son were in our house that night. After I had left you, I snuck in through the kitchens as usual. My father never alerted me to their presence—nor asked me to write a note to you."

His eyes lock on mine, the flames unreadable. Krane's gaze returns to the notes. He looks them both over several times as the silence stretches between us. My heart pounds in my chest. It reaches for him and begs him to believe me. He knows me better than anyone; he has to know, deep down, that I would never betray him like this.

"That cannot be."

His deep voice wavers. For a moment, my heart lifts on a hopeful wind. His shoulders slump as he looks up at me. There is uncertainty in the flames, and I hold my breath. Only for my heart to crumble at his next words.

"This is another one of your lies. Confess now, or you won't like what comes next."

Ice envelopes me as I take in his steely expression. He won't listen to me—he is too angry. There is nothing I can say now that will persuade him of my honesty. My final resort is to lay it all bare and hope that somewhere underneath this twisted form, my Krane is there. It is my only hope for saving both of us.

"I love you, Krane." My voice cracks and tears slide down my cheeks, fresh and hot. "The happiest day of my life was when we handfasted in the woods that glorious night. The moon and the animals of the forest were our only witnesses."

"Stop," he commands, crushing the two notes in his palms.

I press on.

"In my heart, you were always my husband. I vowed to never marry anyone but you, and I meant it."

He looks away, and I hold my breath.

"Then why didn't you leave with me that night?"

I lick my dry lips.

"Because I was afraid," I answer honestly. "Afraid the duke's men would come after us. I knew you didn't have much in the way of money—we never would've been able to outrun them without the funds to travel. I wanted the chance to steal some of my father's gold to help us."

Krane says nothing. His mouth opening remains still. A few green flames flicker and snap, but his body only grows tenser. A lump settles in my throat as I stare at him. I feel the last warm tendrils of his soul slip away from mine. I'm losing him—I've lost him.

For the past month, I've longed to join him in death. Every night, I willed myself to perish to be reunited with him. This is more painful than death. Knowing he is still alive—even in this form—but hates me is too much to bear. I can't go on like this. I was scared before, but clarity finds me in the fog.

With a trembling hand, I find my thigh and unsheath the dagger. There is a flicker of awareness inside the pumpkin.

"What are you doing?" he rasps.

I swallow thickly, lifting the blade. His green flames hypnotize me.

"If you won't believe me—if I've truly lost you to your hatred—then there is no reason for me to linger in this world."

The blade kisses my throat. A trail of warm blood slips from the small knick. I feel the crimson liquid collect along my throat. I suck in one final breath. Memories of my past unravel before me. Each one is beautiful and more bittersweet than the last. Krane is there in all of them, just as he is now, only without the distrust in his eyes.

"Scarlett," he warns, stepping towards me.

I cannot waver. The look in his eyes resigns me to my fate. I try to smile, but the muscles don't work like they should. I haven't used them in a month after all.

"I love you, Krane."

He snarls, stepping closer, but I will not be deterred.

"I love you even if you hate me—my sun. I'd never betray you. I can only pray that my death will prove that to you."

Tears blur my vision, and my hand locks around the hilt of the dagger. Flames pour from Krane's pumpkin—thicker than I've ever seen. He is a glorious creature. I'll tuck the memory of him in this form away with me into whatever world exists beyond this one.

With a steadying breath, the blade presses deeper against me. Before I can make another move, there is the sound of glass shattering, and the whole room erupts in green fire.

13

SCARLETT

Green flames are everywhere.

They lick along the walls of the dungeon and spread along the stone floor. The bars of the cells melt into silver puddles. The temperature reaches an inferno. Sweat beads along my brow. The pumpkin atop Krane's shoulder is no more.

In its place is a skull made entirely of green flames. In an instant, he is across the room, wrenching the knife from my hand and tossing it aside. His flames brush up against me but do not singe my skin. Strong arms wrap around me, and I'm crushed against his powerful chest.

The faint scent of cinnamon nearly sends me to my knees.

His face is solid. Each flame flickers with bewilderment. His eyes are burning with intensity—a madness lurking in their depths. A tremble goes through Krane's body and into mine. I hold tight to him. His warmth soothes the remaining rigidity in my muscles.

"Why would you do that, Scarlett? Why?"

Krane's words are hushed, barely more than a low growl. Tears spill down my cheeks as he pulls me even tighter against him. I feel the hard contours of his body. While he may no longer look like the man I loved, there is no mistaking him. His heart beat pounds in time with my own. The familiar graze of his soul against mine is all I need.

His hands continue their journey over my body. Each harsh touch sends a fire through me. I lean into his body—his hands—willing him to keep touching me and to never stop. Despair flickers in his eyes as he takes a deep breath.

"Have you hurt yourself before?" he whispers.

Tears tumble down my cheeks as I nod.

"After I found you like that..." I swallow soundly, trying to erase the awful memory. "Many times after that day, I tried. I didn't eat—I couldn't."

A shuddering breath rattles his chest. His eyes are still guarded despite the gentle roaming of his hands. Their exploration continues even as I see conflicting emotions war on his face. The flames dance back and forth, twining together to create a look of apprehension and longing. A beautiful maelstrom of loss and longing.

"I don't know what to think," he admits. My breath catches in my throat. "I was so certain of your betrayal. Cursed because of it. After reading that letter, my soul could not find peace. It demanded revenge, and thus my anger forged into this infernal form."

He huffs a humorless laugh. Flames slip from between his lips and ghost over my cheeks.

"I thought that if you confessed and paid for your treachery with your life, I would be returned to my normal body." Krane shakes his head. "At the very least, be allowed to die."

His confession causes my blood to run cold.

"You were going to kill me?"

I shouldn't be surprised, but I can't help it. The idea of my Krane doing such a thing shatters my already fragile heart. The organ has been broken and repaired so many times that I wouldn't be surprised if it gave out.

"When I came to, cursed to be this monster, I was alone. Your betrayal consumed my thoughts. The magic had blighted who I used to be. The anger I died with molded me into this. It tainted every memory—casted every moment into a new light that made your rejection of me make sense." He swallows thickly. "I wanted you to suffer as I had. My need for revenge warped the years we spent together and made me see you as my enemy."

His hands pause on my back, and I take that as a sign. My breath turns sharp in my legs.

"I see," I say, taking a small step back.

Krane's eyes widen as I hold my hands out to my side. Lifting my chin, I meet his gaze.

"If my death will bring you peace, then by all means. I won't stop you. Death would be better than living with your hatred."

Krane growls as green flames lick up the walls. They burn brighter until they are hard to look at. Krane shifts a gloved hand through his flames as if they were hair. An old habit that makes my heart squeeze.

"Nothing makes sense to me now. I want to believe you, but I—"

"You can't," I answer for him.

He is silent for a moment. The sharp line of his mouth turns down. We stare at each other, the room thick with smoke and indecision. My chest rises and falls under his stormy gaze. He seems so far away, yet he stands barely an arm's length away. A sea of distrust crashes between us.

There is only one thing left to do. It is my last-ditch effort— my final card to play in the hopes of changing his mind. I lick my lips, taking a small step closer.

"If you won't believe my words. Maybe you'll believe this."

He eyes me warily as I curl my fingers into his coat. Tugging him forward, I press up onto my toes and seal our mouths together. It feels like coming home. Everything clicks into place inside of me. This is Krane—my Krane. If I had not felt his soul before this kiss would surely solidify who he is to me.

Lips of flames are still against mine. Behind my closed eyes, I can see the flickering of his fire. His face does not burn me. It licks against my skin, warm and inviting as ever. I half expect him to shove me away. To accuse me of using this as another distraction to divert my guilt. His hands remain at his side, and I'm not sure he's breathing.

In an instant, everything changes.

Krane comes alive against my mouth. Snarling into our kiss, his hands grip my back. His fingers tease and trail along the curve of my spine. They sink into my ass, and I gasp against his mouth.

The wet slide of a tongue startles me. Its warm glide along mine causes me to moan. His hands squeeze my flesh. Breaking our kiss, his head falls to my neck, biting and tasting along my sensitive skin. My head falls back, urging him to explore more. How I've missed this—us.

Each touch is familiar; he knows my body better than I do. A thought that is reaffirmed when he nips at my pulse point. My eyes grow heavy, and my mouth opens on a keening moan —moisture slides from me, dampening my inner thighs.

"I'll prove myself to you," I vow.

He groans against me, licking a path up my jaw. His mouth returns to mine as if he can't stop. We're both overcome. My hands sink beneath his coat, gripping his undershirt. I pull at it, desperate to feel his flesh against my hands. His lips leave mine again to pay attention to my cheek. I rub my legs together, desperate for friction.

"I'll earn your trust again," I sigh as he nips my ear. "Together, we'll kill them. They'll confess to their treachery, and you'll see I had no part in any of this."

"Yes," he groans.

Our mouths meet again, biting and devouring each other whole. My body is pressed flat against him, and a seeking hardness strains against my stomach. I moan into our kiss and rub myself against him. I'd gladly let him take me on this stone floor, the rats as our witnesses. I'm overcome. I need him more than anything—without him, I have nothing.

"We'll start with Bram," I say when we break apart again. His fiery eyes flicker. "Then we will kill my father."

"Would you be able to do that? Truly?"

I fuse our mouths, tasting the smokiness in our kiss. His cinnamon scent is spicier than before—wilder. It fills my lungs and my heart. Pulling back, I let him see the truth in my eyes.

"Yes." My edict is final. "For what he did to you. For what he stole from me, his life is forfeit."

With one final searing kiss, Krane pulls back from me. He nods at my words as he rubs a hand through his flames. My lips feel tender. Gently, I lick the bottom one, and I watch his gaze go there. I can see the apprehension back in his eyes. A wall is erected between us, but only this time it has a dozen fractures cracking along it.

I can only hope given more time, I can shatter it fully. We were never meant to be kept apart. I am more certain of that than ever. Krane has lost so much because of me—his life, his humanity. Revenge will be my gift to him. I will do whatever I can to see Bram and my father pay for their crimes against my love.

It will be our duel revenge. They stole my future the moment they cut him down. I could've had everything had their greed not taken it from me. Rage burns inside of me, melting the ice in my veins.

"Tomorrow." Krane's voice cuts through my thoughts, causing me to look up. "Tomorrow, we go after Bram. If what you say is true, I will get him to admit it. Scarlett, I want to believe you I—"

He shakes himself, allowing his hands to fall back to my sides. Giving me a light squeeze, I nearly sag in relief. Krane can't seem to stop touching me, and I never want him to.

"One thing is certain. You need to eat."

At his words, my stomach grumbles loudly. My cheeks burn as I watch his lips twitch in the ghost of a smile. I allow him to pull me up the stairs and hopefully out of the dungeon forever.

Much was revealed tonight, and my mind is a mess of emotions. Confusion, anger, hope—all of them swirl inside me as we walk up into the dark castle. I can't make sense of it all yet. Right now, I know two things. One being that Krane is alive and I still have a chance to build a future with him, albeit one that I never even thought possible. The wife of the Headless Horseman; there are no tales about her spread throughout Broken Cliff.

Secondly, and most importantly, for the first time in a month, I'm hungry.

14

———

THE HEADLESS HORSEMAN

She sleeps soundly on his shoulder.

The feast his magic provided her lies thoroughly devoured atop the fine mahogany table. The Headless Horseman had ensured the food was laced with extra properties to help her gain weight. The supple curves he loved so much had withered into sharp bones.

A few more solid meals, and the damage the last month had done to her would be rectified.

She was already looking better. Color blooms on her delicate cheeks. Her hair has regained some of its usual luster, sparkling in the candlelight. Tendrils of it tickled his cheek as her head rests firmly against his shoulder. Her breaths are deep and even, the swells of her breast rising against the neckline of her gown.

The Headless Horseman had not intended to sit beside her. Nor had he intended to feed her from his hand when she gave a feeble protest that she was full after a few measly bites, just as he had not intended to kiss her in the dungeon.

He licks his lips, stifling a groan.

He can still taste her. Scarlett's lips were as sweet as ever, moving with his in a fever pitch. Kissing her was different in this form—more primal. His blood had boiled at the thought of laying her against the hard floor and taking her roughly. Her sweet, high-pitched moans would break through the last of his resolve, and they would be one again.

Stifling a laugh, he gently shakes his head. He had not intended for any of it, yet he cannot be surprised. She is Scarlett—his Scarlett. The only one he'd do anything for. The one who didn't betray him.

He wants to believe her so badly. There was no hint of deception from her as she showed him the difference between the treacherous note and her vows to that vile earl. Those sterile confessions of love were nothing compared to the ones she'd given him beneath the moon. They may have been written by her hand, but they had not come from her heart.

Glancing down, he sees the small scar on her palm. Removing one of his leather gloves, he takes in the dark gray skin. The long, bony fingers uncurl and reveal the matching scar along his own hand.

Time will tell if she is lying to him. Has his need for revenge warped him enough that he cannot discern truth from reality? Those weeks when he blossomed into this creature were horrible. Rage was his only sustenance. There is a chance that he is wrong about everything. Oh, how he longs for that to be the case.

Earl Bram will reveal the truth when confronted with his death. The young earl is prideful—he will not want to perish to keep up a ruse he didn't want to partake in initially. Surely Scarlett knows that and therefore wouldn't have vowed to kill the earl if she were also complicit in the murder plot.

He regrets killing the duke so quickly, but nothing can be done for that now.

Glancing up at the crumbling ceiling, the moon glows above, flanked by dozens of twinkling stars. It must be very late.

Scarlett's exhaustion is evident. Sleeping inside the dungeon could not have been easy.

Shame swims up his throat, and he nearly chokes on it. In these quiet moments with her warmth seeping into his side, he can admit to truths he'd rather stay hidden. In his heart, buried deep inside the reanimated organ, he longs to take her in his arms again. He wants to apologize to her and tell her he will never doubt her again.

The sight of her with the blade at her throat—the idea that she could leave him behind in this world when they swore never to be parted—undid him. He had traveled through death to be with her again, and he wouldn't allow her to slip through his fingers.

With the moon as his witness, he beseeches it to let all of this be true. Let her innocence be vindicated, and let those who deserve to pay suffer tenfold. If he finds out she was still lying... no, he couldn't even consider it. If this were another betrayal, he would—

Scarlett shifts along his shoulder, moaning softly.

Without thinking, he rises from the table, cradling her in his arms. Her arms go around him instantly as he makes the short journey down the hall. The large bedroom at the end once belonged to a queen. It will be fit enough for Scarlett to sleep in.

His magic has cleansed away the dust and decay. The cobwebs spreading along the walls like lace are wiped clean. The Headless Horseman pushes the double wooden doors open. Their golden hinges groan at the force.

Inside, the room has been restored to its former glory. Fresh paint coats the walls, the marble floor is polished, and the bed is made with fresh satin sheets and adorned with cloud-like pillows. Without preamble, he settles Scarlett atop the soft mattress. She sinks into the welcoming bed.

Her tattered gown contrasts with the fine sheets. Blinking

sleepy blue eyes at him, she rolls around onto her side, groaning softly. Pushing up on her hands, she presents her back to him.

"Help me," she whispers thickly.

The Headless Horseman swallows his chuckle as his fingers make deft work of her corset. After all, he's helped her with her lacings more times than he can count.

Once she is free of the bindings, her stained gown hangs limply from her body. She fights with the cumbersome tiered skirt for a moment, then tosses it onto the floor. Her corset goes next, as does the ribbon around her neck. The dingy fabric flutters to the ground.

Her shoes hit the marble with two thuds. Then, before he can look away, she slides the sleeves of her shift down her arms and kicks the garment away. Her naked body is gloriously revealed in the moonlight. Pale, blue light bathes her. There is no reason for false modesty between them. She is lovely—the most beautiful thing he has ever seen. His mouth goes dry at the sight of her.

The glory of her nudity doesn't last for long as she slips beneath the covers with a sigh. He glances behind him towards the open door. The decision should be easy. It would be unwise to stay when so much still lies unresolved between them.

Scarlett lifts her hand and beckons him closer.

"Stay with me, please," she sighs.

His knees lock in place as he looks at her palm like a lifeline. The silence stretches, and her eyes turn more alert. Her full lips twist into a pout he knows all too well and has never been able to refuse.

"Please. Just until I fall asleep."

He never stood a chance. Grumbling, he settles beside her on the bed. As this creature, he does not need sleep. Sleep was just more suffering—memories from the recesses of his mind sent to torture him.

Cushioned next to Scarlett, he feels at peace for the first time in a month. Her rosewater scent fills his lungs. She curls into his side, laying an arm across his chest, the same way they've fallen asleep together hundreds of times.

His hand raises and threads through her hair. She sighs as he rakes his fingers through the strands—old habits.

"Good night, Krane," she murmurs against his chest, eyelids fluttering closed.

The Headless Horseman knows it is unwise. He should bite his tongue until it bleeds. It's too much and far too soon. The truth will be revealed soon, and if she has been loyal to him, he will make up for all this unpleasantness then.

But he is a weak male, powerless but to succumb to her. It has been that way from the moment they met—it will be that way until he draws his final breath.

"Good night, my moon."

15

SCARLETT

Sunlight streams in through the open window.

Slashes of golden light illuminate my decadent bed. I feel rejuvenated after such a deep and peaceful rest. There's only one sore spot. Even though I shouldn't be surprised, I can't help but be disappointed that I didn't wake to Krane beside me. It seems that no matter how much we had come together last night, there was still work to be done.

He doesn't trust me. Hopefully, tonight will put to bed any more uncertainty he feels towards me, and we can move forward. Together.

Stretching out amongst the sheets, something is different about me. My hands travel along my naked flesh. I gasp at the soft curves that greet my hands. Sharp bones no longer protrude through my skin. Tossing back the covers, I crawl from the bed and walk over to a large mirror propped along the wall.

My reflection shocks me. I no longer look like a stranger. I look like me. Not exactly how I was a month ago, but I'm no longer a wraith barely tethered to this world. My hair shines like a beacon. Dark shadows have been wiped clean from my eyes. My hips and breasts are fuller. Pink decorates my chest and cheeks.

Whatever meal Krane had given me last night had done the trick. His magic can do all. However, I know that it's more than that. Of course, I feel like my old self again. Krane is with me. Everything is just as it should be. Without him, each breath was painful, each day brought forth a new agony. With him, even as the Headless Horseman, I have a reason to live again.

My soul is whole, as is my heart.

Turning from the mirror, I find a dark blue gown hanging from an old wardrobe. Matching slippers rest beneath it. I can't help but smile as I hold the soft fabric. Slipping it over my head, the dress fits me like a glove. The slippers fit perfectly as well. Walking over to a simple vanity, I find a brush and gently untangle my hair. The thought of braiding it crosses my mind, but I decide to leave it down, enjoying its shimmering length.

A soft knocking echoes from the door.

Turning in my seat, I watch the heavy doors push inward to reveal Krane. My heart speeds up at the sight of him. His pumpkin is firmly in place atop his shoulders. Green flames snap and pop inside the openings. They eye me warily as we stand facing each other. The air is thick with tension. While he still doesn't fully trust me, there is a new primal edge between us. I can see the conflicting emotions warring inside of him.

I can only pray that the ones who urged him to kiss me last night prevail.

His soul brushes against mine. Last night, he called me his moon. That has to mean something. This wall of ice between us will be smashed into splinters by tonight. I will make sure of it.

It's almost funny to watch us. The two people who always knew exactly what to say to each other at all times seem not to understand how to navigate this new dynamic. The silence stretches until Krane finally clears his throat—clarity dances in his green flames.

"Would you like breakfast?"

I nod eagerly; my stomach is already rumbling. After feasting the night before, the days I spent in hunger come rearing back. I will gorge myself to make up for lost time. I no longer wish to resemble the ghost I was becoming. I want to live with Krane by my side.

Krane extends a gray hand towards me. He has removed his gloves, and now I can see the state of his hands. The skin is rough, as if burned. Dark nails decorate the tips of his fingers. However, I don't hesitate to take his hand in mine. He is my Krane; while he may look different, he feels just the same to me.

He leads me from the room and we walk down a carpeted hallway towards the dining room, where we were the previous evening. Once inside, he guides me to the upholstered chair I occupied before, and he settles in beside me, much to my delight.

The room is just the same. Crumbling wallpaper and dust-covered paintings line the walls. A glistening mahogany table is laden with all manner of breakfast items. Steam curls over the lips of silver serving dishes. Fluffy scrambled eggs are arranged artfully next to crispy bacon. Golden biscuits rest inside a tea towel. Jars of jam and pots of fresh butter rest beside them.

My heart stumbles in my chest as I look at the color of the jam—blackberry—my favorite. Of course it is, Krane's magic made this feast. I look shyly over to him, only to find his eyes already on me. My throat suddenly feels tight. I clear it before lifting my plate and spooning all manner of delicious food onto the porcelain.

Once I have taken bits of everything, I notice Krane does not reach for his own plate. After buttering a warm biscuit, I slather a thick spread of glossy jam atop it. Glancing up at Krane, I nod towards his plate.

"Do you no longer have to eat?"

A beat of silence passes before he nods.

"I'm not human anymore. All of those urges have been blighted."

Lifting the biscuit to my lips, I pause before taking a bite.

"All of them?"

Krane watches me, his green flames flickering quickly inside his eye holes. His gaze snags on my lip as I lick a piece of jam from the corner of my mouth.

"Most of them."

I swallow soundly. This is the most we've talked since our reunion. I don't want to fall back into tense silence.

"How does the magic work?"

Krane sighs, shrugging his massive shoulders.

"I don't really know. When I was made into this," he pauses to gesture down at himself, "there was fire and pain—a cleansing and reforging of my soul. Memories were stolen for a time. I was unmade and twisted into this creature. Revenge was my sole motivation—it was the only tangible thing I had. The anger was all I could remember."

I stop my chewing, the food turning to ash in my mouth. Krane's eyes sharpen.

"I don't say this to upset you. In truth, I have no idea why I was made into this. At my creation, there were only whispers. Whatever force transformed me led me to believe that it could be undone somehow. If my revenge was satiated, then perhaps there was a chance." His lips twist. "Unfortunately, there's no guidebook on how to be the Headless Horseman of Broken Cliff. Everything—including the magic—has been things I've learned through trial and error. If I think of something, I can make it appear. I can transform myself into different forms. There are limits to my powers, of course. I find a new one every day."

I nod at his explanation. My appetite returns at his urging, and I spear a piece of egg with my silver fork. It melts against my tongue like butter. How strange that he does not know his purpose for being here. Whatever created him must've done so for a purpose. Perhaps my prayers had been answered, albeit in a cruel way. I begged for him to come back to me, and someone—or something—had heard me and answered.

I would be grateful for Krane no matter how I had him. I abhor his pain, but I cannot be angry that we've been given a second chance together.

Glancing around the room, I lift a brow at him.

"Where are we exactly?"

"Nightingale Castle."

I nearly choke on my final slice of bacon. Coughing, I take a sip of water before wiping at the grease decorating my mouth.

"Tell me you're kidding."

Something like amusement flickers in his flames. His mouth twists.

"Don't tell me you're afraid of ghosts, Scar."

I narrow my eyes at his jibe even as my heart squeezes at the use of that nickname. No one but him calls me that. I take another biscuit and coat it in jam. Turning towards him, I shake my head.

"Regardless of ghosts, you know the stories about this place. A mad king who slaughtered his whole family. It's said to be—"

"Cursed?" Krane points a long finger at his pumpkin head. "I think we're well past that."

I fight not to roll my eyes.

"Regardless, no one travels this deep into the *Whispering Woods*. Lest you wish to lose your mind and become a meal for whatever manner of bloodthirsty creatures dwell here."

"Look at me. I'm quite the deterrent for anything that would seek to do either of us harm."

When I still don't look convinced, he shrugs. He takes the other half of my biscuit and spreads jam on it.

"When I first changed, I needed a place to heal. This seemed as good a place as any."

He sets the biscuit on my plate.

"Oh, no. I can't. It's too much—"

"Eat," he commands.

I do as he says, still ravenously hungry. He observes me, taking in every bite.

"No one would happen upon me here. I could regenerate in peace."

"You were always fond of your alone time."

Krane throws his head back, a rusty laugh escaping him—my heart pounds at the familiar sound.

"I rarely got any. Between my responsibilities around the manor and you, I barely had a moment of peace."

Biting into my biscuit, I roll my eyes.

"You poor thing. Was being with me really such a chore?"

Krane stares at me as I sit back in my chair after polishing off the last bite of biscuit. I am stuffed now. I feel as if I will burst out of my gown. Krane lifts a tentative hand, and I hold my breath. His thumb drifts to the corner of my mouth. Thumbing away a lingering bit of jam, I watch as his thick tongue snakes out from his mouth hole and licks it from his finger.

I suppress a shiver—moisture slicks between my thighs.

"A chore? No." His eyes gleam with mischief. "Exhausting? Yes."

I raise a brow.

"I don't recall you complaining."

Krane huffs a laugh, flames slipping from his mouth.

"Who would complain about receiving a gift they've always wanted—even if that gift demands my full enthusiasm, even after toiling away in the stables from dawn to dusk."

My lips lift into a grin.

"And enthusiastic you always were."

The lightness between us is familiar. We were always like this—bantering back and forth, calling each other's bluffs. Always quick to share a laugh. If this were before, we'd already be naked. With a whole castle to ourselves and no one looking for us, we'd never be able to pull ourselves apart.

Even with the levity between us, I can see the separation that remains. That wall of ice is the only barrier between our hearts. His gaze becomes more guarded, smothering his good-humored smirk into a straight line.

I'm desperate to keep it from forming further.

"Do you remember my old tutor, Madam Bovery?"

He nods, confused.

"The one from up north, with the yellowing teeth and that always smelled like creek water?"

I can't help but laugh.

"The very one. God, she was awful. No child ever gave her as much grief as you did."

Krane shrugs.

"I was ten. What ten-year-old wants to spend his summer afternoons in a dusty study reading over spelling books?"

"You were a terrible student." Color warms my cheeks. "But I loved when you would attend lessons."

"Because it made you look even more perfect than normal?"

I smack at his shoulder, and his eyes go to the feather-light touch.

"No. It was nice not to be alone with her."

His eyes flicker with awareness.

"Her lessons were the first time you ever spoke to me."

I nod, licking along my bottom lip.

"I remember."

The memories come rushing back. Madam Bovery had been cruel to me over my poor penmanship. Krane had been dismissed halfway through the lesson, only to discover me crying in my father's field later. He had made me laugh and told me that Madam Bovery was a miserable old woman who was only a tutor so that she could torment children. Krane had sat beside me until my mother called me in for dinner.

I had forgotten all about Madam Bovery's biting critique by the next day. Krane had not. Instead, he had found a toad from the manor's pond and hid it under her stack of lessons.

"I can still hear her screams after discovering the poor, slimy creature," I say. I wrinkle my nose. "Though her forcing you to write *I will not terrorize Madam Bovery with amphibians ever again.*' all day for the next three weeks seemed like an extreme punishment."

Krane's eyes turn soft.

"It made you laugh. It was worth it."

The air between us shifts as we stare at each other—the memories of the past play over and over. Wherever I was, Krane was there too as my friend, my protector, and finally as my lover. Reaching up, I capture his hand in mine. My thumb traces the bumpy skin along the back of his palm.

"I want it to stay like this between us."

Immediately, the tenderness ices over. His expression turns guarded, but I hold fast.

"Tonight will answer everything. You will see that I never betrayed you—that you can trust me."

Krane says nothing, but he does give my hand one hard squeeze before pulling away. I reluctantly let him go. I sit back in my chair, taking in the fading light. I must have slept later than I thought, as the sun is already on the other side of the horizon.

"Do you have a plan for tonight?"

Krane huffs, waving a dismissive hand.

"Show up. Scare the earl. Threaten him. Get his confession." His green flames dance. "Kill him."

Simple enough, yet foolish. I shake my head.

"It won't be that easy. He'll have his father's guards—more

than he had to oversee our wedding." Krane seems to want to argue, but I push on. "The king may have even sent his own forces. If we want to get close to Bram, then we have to find a way inside. One that won't send him running at the first hint of danger."

Krane is quiet for a moment. His mouth twists as if digesting my words. I hold my breath—awaiting his dismissal. Instead, he merely nods, eyes turning sharp.

"Did you have something in mind?"

A smile curves my lips. I, too, have had time to plot my revenge against the earl for the part he played in Krane's slaying.

"I had one idea."

16

THE HEADLESS HORSEMAN

Her plan had worked flawlessly.

She was far more clever than he—always had been. Her idea to show up dressed as his missing bride, wracked with a barrage of tears, had fooled the guards enough to let her pass. Little did they know he was concealed within her shadow, following closely behind as she babbled incoherently. The guards swiftly led her into Earl Bram's chambers, shutting the door quickly so as not to have to hear anymore of her wailing.

The young earl had been shocked to see her. The whiskey glass had shattered at his feet as he stood. He did not send her away—did not even seem to notice her tears drying instantly along her cheeks. The Headless Horseman could hardly blame him. She was a vision in white.

There was no doubt that Earl Bram would forgo any inquiry about their gruesome wedding day and where she had spent the last week in order to bed her.

That would not be happening.

The moment the door shut behind the final guard, the Headless Horseman had revealed himself from under her white cloak. Bram screamed, but it was of no use. His guards could not save him now as green fire flowed around the room, barring the door. Falling to his knees, Earl Bram bows his head in supplication.

"I beg you. Mercy."

Arrogant fool, he will pay for his part in this. Snarling, he reaches down and pulls Bram's head back. His gaze burns the other man alive.

"Do you know who I am?"

"Please—Please let me go. Let me—"

"Answer me!"

Bram begins to wail in earnest. The scent of urine permeates the room. A weak male, he was never worthy of a woman like Scarlett. He couldn't keep her safe—would surely never satisfy her.

"No!" Bram screams. "I have no idea. Please!"

"Think," Scarlett snaps. "I know it's not something you're used to doing."

His gaze turns towards her. Hatred swims in his eyes. Baring his teeth, he moves to lunge for her, unable to, thanks to the Headless Horseman's firm grip.

"You bitch! This is all your fault!"

Another growl rips through him as he catches Bram around the throat. In a flash, he pins the other man to the wall. Blood smears behind his head. His flames lick against the other man, burning his clothes. The green fire would never hurt Scarlett, but Bram is another story.

"This is your fault!" Scarlett screams. "You killed him."

Bram groans as the Headless Horseman keeps him locked in his grasp. Pain radiates from him. Confusion makes his mouth tilt at the corner.

"Who?"

"The love of my life."

It still doesn't click for Bram. He thrashes against the Headless Horseman's palm, but it is useless. After a few more moments of struggling, it seems to click for him. He looks at Scarlett, contempt dripping from his tongue.

"That poor stable boy? Is that what this is about?"

"Yes," he snarls into Bram's face. "You made me into this."

Bram's eyes flicker between him and Scarlett. His feet barely touch the stone floor. Sweat breaks out along his forehead as the green flames loom closer. Licking his lips, it's apparent he thinks he can lie his way out of this one. There will be nothing but the truth uttered in this room.

"Confess to the plot, Bram," Scarlett urges. "Or he will start hurting you. Worse."

As if to make her point, one of his flames licks along the earl. It burns away his clothing, exposing the pale flesh of his right thigh to the heat. Bram screams and writhes. The flames hover close, not enough to burn but enough to be uncomfortable. The threat is clear. His only chance at salvation is if he reveals the whole truth.

Bram remains tight-lipped, so the Headless Horseman urges his flames closer. His skin begins to blister and boil. Bram screams as the scent of burning flesh fills the air. He guides his flames against his ruined flesh again. Then again, until the earl finally buckles.

"Okay! Okay! I'll tell you what you want to know. Please just stop."

The flames pull back, but only a fraction. Bram rests his sweaty head against the stone wall of his chambers. His white undershirt is soaked in perspiration.

"The truth about that night," the Headless Horseman demands.

Bram swallows thickly.

"It was her father's idea."

Glancing towards Scarlett, he sees the anger in her eyes. The depth of her father's betrayal had surprised her just as it had him. This is it, the moment of truth. For all the lies to be laid bare from the lips of one arrogant earl. He will do anything to save himself; there would be no reason to lie. Not when he is exactly where they want him.

"Everyone knew you'd been fucking the stable boy. It was hardly a secret. None of the other lords had wanted to marry you because of it. Who wants a spoiled bride?"

Flames erupt along his leg, burning his skin down to the bone. His scream rips through the room.

"Apologize," the Headless Horseman demands through clenched teeth.

"I'm sorry. I'm sorry!"

He shouts the words at Scarlett, who rolls her eyes. She never cared about the gossip about them. If it had been a shield that kept the suitors away for as long as it did, then he was grateful for the whispers. After all, they were true. She was not spoiled—she was his.

"When my father sought your hand for me, he knew these rumors would be a problem. If the stable boy was allowed to live, the legitimacy of my heirs would always be called into question." Bram takes a deep, shuddering breath. "Not to mention, if he were still alive, there was a chance you'd flee with him. My father had already paid a high price for you and was desperate. He wouldn't let anything jeopardize his investment. Nor would your father allow anything to prevent more gold from entering his coffers. He knew the stable boy could not be allowed to live and thus sent him on his fool's errand that night."

Bram laughs without humor, shaking his head.

"Folk tradition, he had said. Collect the pumpkin of the headless rider. An impossible task. It was only meant to lure him deep in the *Whispering Woods* so that your father could kill him out there with no witnesses." Bram sneers at her. "Poor bastard. His love for you made him oblivious to the danger.

Asking for your hand in front of me and my father was the final insult. He was always going to die; that night just presented the easiest way for it to be accomplished."

Silvery tears fall down her cheeks, but she hastily wipes them away. Her eyes are two blue flames. Scarlett is lovely and fierce—heartbreakingly beautiful.

"Tell him I had nothing to do with it. Tell him I never wanted to be with you," Scarlett demands.

The breath stills in his lungs. This is it, the final piece to slide into place. The earl has the chance to end his suffering and absolve her. He has admitted to everything thus far. The Headless Horseman hoped two didn't have to fall tonight.

"Be with me?" Bram scoffs. "You hated me. I could tell from our first meeting that this marriage would not be easy. If we even managed to get you down the aisle, my father swore we'd have to tie you to the marriage bed if there was any hope in consummating it. I was afraid you'd kill me before I even got the chance to try and give you an heir."

"I would've," Scarlett spits.

She looks pleased, but there is one lingering bit of the story that still remains at large. His palms bite into Bram's shoulder, squeezing painfully. The earl wheezes against the discomfort.

"And the note? Who was responsible for that?"

Bram looks confused, but a fresh gliding of flames against his ruined skin helps him remember.

"The note! Yes, the *note*. Her mother wrote it." He tries to shrug to no avail. "She urged her husband to let him go—that he was just a simple stable boy—but she wrote it nonetheless. Handed it over with little care in the end. I don't know why Richard insisted on it. He was a sadistic man. Probably only did it to hurt the poor bastard even more—punishment for nearly thwarting his plans to marry her off."

The words wash over the Headless Horseman like a balm. He hears them for what they are—the truth in each statement is exactly as Scarlett recounted it. She hadn't betrayed him. She was loyal to him this whole time, and he had thrown her in the dungeon and tormented her with visions of the worst moment of her life. He had been cruel to her—threatened to kill her.

All that he had done replays before him. It is her love for him that keeps her at his side. She had a chance to escape but never took it. Being with him, even as this creature, mattered more to her than being alone. She was beautiful and kind. And his. Shame floods him. Guilt casts what he's done in a harsh light. His need for revenge had twisted him into something he hadn't recognized.

He knew her better than anyone—had loved her for as long as he could remember. He should've believed she had no part in this. The letter was an apparent forgery; there were plenty of indications of it that he had chosen to ignore. He would never question her again.

The mistakes he made would be atoned for tonight and for every night they shared together after this. There would be no questioning his devotion for as long as she drew breath. He would never hurt again—he would safeguard her heart and soul. He would beg for her forgiveness and lay himself bare to her.

The Headless Horseman finds Scarlett's eyes. They are clear as they meet his gaze. She gasps at whatever flickers in his flames. Their future begins tonight.

"Let me go!" Bram demands. "I've told you what you wanted to hear."

Tearing his eyes away from Scarlett is a feat, but he manages.

"No."

The simple word echoes around the room. Bram opens his mouth, but it is far too late to put up a fight. Hooking his large hands around the earl's head, the Headless Horseman twists with force. Flesh tears and muscles rip. A chorus of shredding tendons and cracking bones follows. The earl screams until he is silenced forever.

The Headless Horseman tosses the earl's head to the ground with little care. Crimson spreads out along the floor, but he pays it little mind. Turning towards Scarlett, her gaze is not on the gore but on him. Wide and devastatingly blue.

Does she fear him now? Has she glimpsed his brutality and now wishes to turn away from him? With her truth confirmed, he would deserve her rejection. She doesn't give it, merely lifts her hand towards him, ignoring her intended rotting at their feet.

"Take me home."

Of course, she would not fear him. She knows him better than anyone—loves him even as a vile monster that kept her caged. She was always loyal to him, and he will never doubt her devotion again.

The past haunted him. It twisted all of his memories into hateful scenarios. He had spent so long dwelling on what had happened, but that could be put aside for the night. He had a woman to take care of. His Scarlett would never doubt his devotion again.

Taking her in his arms, he whisks her away from the gruesome scene. She cuddles into him without delay. He breathes in her floral scent and lets it wash over him. There is still another that has to pay for his part in all of this, and he will, but there has been enough vengeance for the past tonight.

Now, he wants to focus solely on his future.

17

SCARLETT

The journey back to Nightingale Castle is different. There had been tension between Krane and me at breakfast, but that is nothing compared to the unspoken words lingering between us now. My back is crushed against his chest as his horse carries us deep into the forest—his heartbeat pounds against my shoulder. One hand grips the reins while the other rests against my stomach, holding me firmly to him.

I relax back against his body as the events of the night play out.

It had been pleasing watching Bram die. After he confirmed my story—that I had no part in Krane's murder—I was happy to see him meet a painful end. It was what he deserved after all. The same fate would soon await my father. I stop myself from getting lost in another revenge fantasy. There will be time later to make them pay.

For now, I can focus on Krane. We can make up for all the lost time. I saw it in his eyes after Bram's confession. The icy wall of apprehension that once stood before us had melted away in Bram's chamber. Our future was certain again. No matter what he looked like, he was my Krane, and we would never be apart again.

There is no place for sadness and betrayal. Not when we both still draw breath. I feel it in his touch as we navigate the uneven terrain. Branches whip overhead as we race through the dark woods. Night air burns my lungs, the faint traces of cinnamon making my heart pound.

Finally, after what feels like hours, the horse trots to a stop outside the crumbling castle. Krane slides from the animal and lowers me to the ground with two hands on my waist. The grand structure is decomposing with time. Legend says it was a wedding gift to a queen. The spirits of the forest had not been pleased with the castle invading their home, so they drove her husband mad.

He killed his whole family before disappearing into the woods, never to be seen again. I shake myself from the gruesome story. The night air causes goosebumps to break out along my exposed flesh. The scent of pine is everywhere. The lace sleeves barely cover my arms, and the heavy satin does nothing to ward off the chill.

Krane leads me inside. The statues along the entryway are cracked and covered in thick cobwebs. Inside, the front room is just as deteriorated as the exterior. My hands trail along the bare walls, disrupting decades' worth of dust. Krane lingers behind me.

Reaching the grand staircase, I look up. Leaves fall in from the crumbling roof as the moon glows above. Climbing the first two steps, I pause and turn towards Krane. Our eyes are level with one another. He breathes deeply, green flames casting his face in jagged shadows.

"Are you hungry?"

My stomach feels empty, but it is not food I desire. I simply shake my head no.

"Tired?"

Again, I shake my head, not trusting my voice.

His large hands find their way to my waist. He skims up and down my sides, causing me to sigh. The green flames dim as his mouth turns down. Squeezing the flesh of my hips, his voice is barely above a whisper.

"Can you ever forgive me, Scarlett?" The devastation in his eyes nearly sends me to my knees. "For locking you up, for doubting you, for letting my need for revenge twist the beautiful life we shared."

Moisture burns my eyes, but I quickly blink it away. My hands cup his face, skimming along the smooth surface of the pumpkin. Tracing each groove, I smile at him.

"There is nothing to forgive."

Krane shakes his head while dragging me closer.

"I should've come for you once I was strong enough. Taken you from your parents' home and kept you safe with me. If you had hurt yourself—died because of me—all the while I was sitting here plotting how to make you hurt just as much as I had…" He trails off, swallowing thickly. "I never would've been able to live with myself. I don't know if I can die in this form, but I would've tried. Anything to have been reunited with you."

"Never mind that," I sigh. "We are together now. The past is the past."

Unease flickers in his eyes. The scent of cinnamon and cloves wraps around me like a blanket. I want to devour him whole—to fuse our bodies together so there is no separating us. His hands pause on my waist.

"How can you still want me? I am a grotesque monster—nothing like the man you once loved."

My hand leaves his face. I make short work of the buttons of his coat. His breathing turns heavy as I bear his undershirt. Unlacing it, I press my palm against the smooth skin of his chest. The strong beat of his heart travels up my arm and enters my own racing organ.

"You look just the same to me. Your heart and soul are the same. I can feel them both reaching towards mine."

His hand comes down atop mine. Gently lifting it from his skin, he turns it over. Tracing the faded scar with his thumb, his eyes heat. It's the same one he has along his palm.

"This was the happiest night of my life. I'd never seen anyone as beautiful as you in your white frock." Fiery eyes trace the planes of my face. "It seems impossible for you to look even lovelier tonight."

I thread our fingers together. His hand is nearly double the size of mine. I curl our palms together and lean forward, trapping our hands against both of our hearts.

"We can be together again, just like we were that night." Krane sucks in a breath as my breasts pillow between us. "There is no one here to stop us. No finite amount of time we have to fight against. It is just you and me now. Alone."

"That's all I've ever wanted, Scar."

My forehead presses against the cool, waxy surface of the pumpkin. The love I feel for him is reflected in his dancing flames.

"Then let us not be apart any longer."

Without another word, Krane scoops me up under my knees and hauls me against him. I giggle as he rushes us up the grand staircase. His steps slow as we push into my bedroom. The sheets and pillows have been refreshed. Depositing me atop the soft mattress, I stare up at him.

Krane is quite the foreboding figure. Taller than he was as a human and stronger, too. His pumpkin head seeps with fire. It is sentient, twisting with each emotion playing across his face. He shakes his head, looking away from me.

"I am hideous, Scarlett. I will give you pleasure, but my needs can be forgotten. I wouldn't subject you to such a thing."

The self-loathing in his eyes breaks my heart. How can he say that about himself? Yes, he looks different. A pumpkin for a head and gray skin are not exactly normal. However, he is not unappealing. His appearance took some getting used to, but now that I have, I see him for who he is. I welcome him in any form. This is better than never having him again.

Rising up, I grip the lapels of his coat and pull him down on top of me. His weight is more than before, but the feel of his body atop mine is familiar. I revel in it. Spreading my legs as wide as my gown will allow, I welcome him closer to my body. If he reaches under my skirts, he can determine for himself just how badly I want him.

The wetness coating my thighs is more than enough evidence.

"You will deny me no part of yourself," I say. "I want all of you, just as you are."

With no more words needed on the matter, I seal our mouths together. The firm skin of the pumpkin is shocking at first. The flames I had kissed before had molded to my mouth. After a moment, the pumpkin does the same. It fits perfectly to my lips and feels as though I am kissing warm, thick skin. Small miracles.

His tongue licks into my mouth, and I groan. It wrestles with mine for a moment before I give in. Over and over, he tastes me, my hips rising to rub against him. He groans into my mouth, yanking me forward on the bed.

Making quick work of my laces, after all, he is an expert at removing my clothes, my white gown hangs from me. Together, our hands knock as we remove it from my body. The only clothing that remains is a pair of simple white stockings. I moan as Krane's fingers hook into them, gently dragging them down my legs and pressing kisses to my pink knees.

He falls on top of me with a groan. There is a feverishness to his mouth that is new. A primal edge that gives way to his desperate touch. As a human, my couplings with Krane were more than pleasurable, but he was simply a man then. Now he is part creature. With all his other human urges done away with, his desire has run rampant, taken to animalistic peaks.

I rub my wetness against the front of his tenting trousers. I want to see more of him—desirous for him to be as naked as I am. My hands go to his coat, pushing it off his shoulders and untucking his white shirt. I toss it aside. Gray skin covered in a menagerie of bumps greets my eyes—his heart-shaped birthmark dances on his flesh. I gently trace it, and Krane moans.

His mouth descends down my chest. Stopping at my left breast, he wraps his lips around my hard nipples. My head pushes back against the soft mattress.

"Krane," I sigh.

Flames lick along my skin, causing goosebumps to break out along my flesh. He releases my breast with a pop, eyes glowing with lust.

"You taste sweeter than ever, Scar."

I grind myself against him as he gives my other nipple the same treatment. His other hand skims down my stomach before stopping between my thighs. I groan as he traces a long finger up my slit. Coating his fingers in my arousal, he gently tucks one into my entrance. My teeth clench together. His fingers are larger, spearing into me deeper than ever before. Stars dance in my vision.

"I never thought I'd have this again. If it wasn't with you, it would be with no one. We are each other's only. Forever."

Krane nods against my breast, sheathing another finger inside me. He curls them just the way I like, making my hips lift from the bed. He hisses against my skin, fiery eyes finding mine.

"Your pussy missed me. I may be a monster, but she recognizes me all the same. Knows I am her master. The only one who gets to worship her." He pumps me harder, adding a third finger. "How did your pretty cunt manage to get even tighter?"

My vision turns dark around the edges. Pleasure wraps

around me with both hands. The sloppy sounds of his fingers fucking me are more than I can bear. My muscles coil tightly as I clench down around his thrusting hand.

"Krane," I groan.

"Let me hear you, Scarlett. I no longer have to quiet your moans with a hand over your mouth—biting my palm to keep from screaming my name." A primal smile curls his lips. "Let me hear what I do to you. Soak me with your come. I need to taste it."

My peak looms, and when Krane's head goes between my thighs to join his fingers, I'm done for. The first lick of his tongue against my clit sends me into bliss. My thighs squeeze his pumpkin head until I'm sure it will crack. His slippery tongue unfurls, longer than possible, and licks the whole length of me. I do as he asks and scream his name, words of pleasure falling from my lips.

"Krane, yes! I'm close—so close. Oh!"

With one final expert curl of his fingers, and with his lips sucking on my clit, my body erupts. Every nerve comes alive, and every muscle tightens. Flames break out along my skin as I scream through my release. It is probably more prolonged after having been denied for the past month. Tears sting my eyes as I finally manage to come down. Krane removes his fingers, his tongue spearing into my entrance to lick up every drop of my spend.

My thighs tremble as he prowls back up my body, limply dangling around his hips. Warm lips find mine as he shares my taste.

"You were worth risking death over. That sweet little pussy sent me to my grave. It belongs to me as do you."

"Always," I vow, taking his mouth in another fevered kiss.

He kisses me again before pulling back. I slide up the bed and prop myself up on my elbows. Pink colors my chest and cheeks. My stomach quivers in anticipation as I watch his hands go to his trousers. There is a tremble to his fingers as he goes to undo the lacings.

"Are you sure you want this, Scarlett? I am no longer a man —things about me have changed."

I smile at him, propping up my knees and exposing myself fully to his hungry gaze. His eyes roam over me as if seeing me for the first time. I spread my thighs even wider, my invitation more than clear.

"I want you inside me, Krane. Would you so easily deny me?"

Krane growls, fisting the waistband of his pants.

"I've never been able to say no to you."

With one tug, his pants fall to the floor, and he kicks them away. I gasp as my mouth grows dry. He wasn't kidding; he isn't a man anymore. The proud flesh that greets my eyes is nearly the length of my forearm. His pale gray shaft is decorated with slight ridges that mirror those of the pumpkin. The head is darker gray, already leaking a pearl of seed—my mouth waters at the sight.

More moisture leaks from my intimate flesh as I imagine what he will feel like inside of me. He takes himself in his hand, spreading his come over the tip and giving himself a rough pump.

"I told you," he says, clearly taking my gasp as one of apprehension.

"The only thing I'm worried about is how you're going to fit all that inside of me."

His mouth flattens into a line.

"I won't hurt you," he vows.

"I know. But that doesn't mean I don't want to try and take as much of you as I can."

Krane groans, pumping himself roughly.

"Wanton woman, what am I going to do with you?"

"Fuck me." I bat my eyelashes at him. "Please."

"You and your fucking please's," he grumbles while crawling up my body.

We both hold our breath as he fits his head to my entrance. My wetness allows him to glide in easily. Hard, gray flesh disappears into my pink opening. He's barely inside me, and the stretch is already significant. My head falls back against my shoulders.

It is a reunion and rebirth all at once. We were torn apart, and now at least we have come together. We will be something new after tonight—something unbreakable. His hands fall to my hips to keep me steady. His invasion is slow, holding himself tightly to keep from impaling me all at once.

He doesn't stop, not until my ass presses against the cradle of his hips. The feel of him is amazing—familiar and yet entirely different. The ridges of his cock cause my eyes to roll back in my head. The hard length of him is burning hot, pulsing with awareness. It is a tight fit, and I feel blissfully full. Of him—Krane. My heart, once a mess of jagged pieces, is whole again. Our souls weave together into a tapestry of forever. I let our lovemaking take me to another world.

My legs lift and wrap around his hips, pulling him even deeper. My nails shred down the skin of his back. He groans, pulling his hips back and pumping into me again. Fire spills from inside the pumpkin. His face is twisted. In pain or pleasure, I cannot be sure.

"So fucking tight, Scarlett. I can't believe they sought to take this away from me. I will kill them all for denying such bliss—for denying me you."

"Krane," I moan. "Move. Make love to me. Erase the scars of the past and claim me for all time."

He retreats his hips before thrusting into me again. I moan in pleasure, but Krane only curses. Flames spill from him as his hands tremble on the sheet beside me.

"Scarlett, I—the rage. I don't know what to do with it. It's what made me into this. It's always here, blanketing everything else. I worry that if I let myself get too carried away..."

He shakes his head, not wanting to finish.

Lifting myself from the bed, I find his mouth.

"Unleash it on me," I say against his lips.

He swiftly shakes his head.

"No, I couldn't."

"I can take it, Krane. I want it—all of you." Our mouths meet again. "Fuck all of your rage into me. Let my body absolve you from it."

Krane growls, pulling back until he nearly withdraws from me. He slams back into me with a sharp slap of our bodies. My breasts bounce at the force, and euphoria unlocks inside me. Our lovemaking was always tender in the past, but we are not the same people we were a month ago. This desperation burns us both alive. I will not have him holding any part of himself back from me. I want to be burned alive by his anger —a vessel for his absolution. He can use me however he wishes, knowing that only pleasure awaits me on the other side.

He fucks into me again, and my teeth clench together.

"Yes," I moan. "Harder. Faster."

Krane does it again, his hands holding my hips a loft so he can power into me. Green flames flow down his shoulders. They glide against my skin.

"Leave no question who owns me. Mark me inside and out."

He growls at me, continuing to fuck me unrestrained. The muscles of his shoulders tense as he pounds into me. His fingers are turning white against my skin, and I'll no doubt have bruises there in the morning. My mouth opens on a pant. Each glide of his rigids along my inner walls sends my body hurting towards another climax. His cinnamon scent only encourages my pleasure.

Slamming into me again, his balls graze against my ass.

Lifting my legs over his shoulders, he nearly folds me in half. The angle is much deeper this way; his face hovers above mine.

"You are my madness, Scarlett. From the moment we met, all my thoughts were of you." He pushes my hips further back to take me deeper, rougher. "When I was young, I'd stand below your window at night, for any sight of you. I contemplated ways to sneak into your room—to take you just as I am now. Never thought you'd seek me out on your own. Never thought I'd get to feel this perfect pussy around my cock."

"Krane," I groan.

He licks up my sweaty cheek, hysteria dancing in his flames. He is Krane, but he is also the Headless Horseman. A monster more powerful than I can comprehend. It is no longer only a man who desires me but a creature who demands a primal claim on me. I welcome it all, only praying that I survive the climax that is about to unmake me.

"I dreamed of taking you in your bed. Your screams of pleasure waking the house. Your father would discover us and have no choice but to wed you to me. Even if he had tried to separate us, I would've found a way." His lips find my ear, my thighs pressing into my chest. "He did discover us that day. Didn't he, Scarlett? He had said nothing as I took you. I heard him leave, but honestly, he could've stayed and watched for all I cared. Nothing would ever make me leave your cunt."

"Oh my god, Krane! I'm close, I'm—"

My eyes glaze over at his crude declaration. The truth of it settles into my bones. My father had discovered us that day and we hadn't stopped. Though he hadn't stayed around to watch, we had made no moves to separate, to feel even an ounce of shame for having been caught. It was wicked, but it was the truth.

Krane snarls as he tosses my legs from his shoulders. I can barely catch my breath as he hooks me around my knees and tosses me face down. Hoisting me up under my hips, I groan as he kneels behind me and licks up both my holes. I scream into the sheets as his tongue gently prods my back entrance.

"Sweeter than honey," he sighs. "Food tastes like ash in my mouth, but your sweetness cannot be denied."

I prop myself up on my elbows, tilting my head to the side. His hardness tucks into my folds and enters me in one thrust. I moan into the sheets, gripping them between my white knuckles.

"If only you could see how well you take my cock. This is what you were born to do." He chuckles darkly, snatching my hair in his fist until my back bows to him. "They wanted you to be a noble lady, but that could never be your role. You're too wanton—passionate. You need to be fucked, Scarlett. Those weak lords never could've satisfied you."

"Yes!"

My breasts jostle as he pounds into me.

"You needed someone strong. Someone who would put you in your place. That's why you sought me out in the stables, knew I was the only man who could satisfy your tight holes. Isn't that right?"

I nod frantically. His hand whips through the air and connects with my ass. The bite of pain heightens my arousal. Wetness coats my inner thighs and drips onto the bed below. My breath catches as he fucks me even harder. His hips press against my tender flesh, and I can barely breathe.

"This is your place, Scarlett. Not the lady of some manor, not some stuffy duchess—you are mine. Your place is in our bed, where I can fuck you long and hard. Forever."

"You always had such a filthy mouth." My words slur.

I moan as he snatches my head back even further. Another sharp smack is delivered to my other ass cheek, then the other. Over and over until pain radiates from both. My climax looms, and I clench down tightly on his thrusting cock. Krane snarls behind me. His fingers grip my hips to leverage himself more into me.

"Do that again and I'll flood your little cunt with my seed. Enough that it'll drip from you until morning."

A delicious shiver runs through me. His cinnamon scent fills my lungs.

"Please, I want it."

My voice is a breathy pout. Krane's hand flattens on my back and pushes me into the mattress. He fucks me deeply, tickling the hidden spot within me he's always been able to find. Our bodies slap together in the symphony of love. Each thrust is a beautiful mix of pleasure and pain.

"Scream for me, Scarlett."

I do as he says. With one hand sneaking under my hips, he works my clit in tight, fast circles. My breath catches in my throat, and I'm thrown from this world into the next. Flames dance over my skin, and everything around me melts away.

This climax is different from all the others he's given me before. It is truly the beginning of what the future holds for us. It binds us together; every part of us is connected. Especially as Krane thrusts into me once, twice, then goes still with a chest-rattling groan. He falls along my sweaty back as he releases torrents of his warm seed inside of me. There is so much it spills out of me and coats my inner thighs.

He rings himself dry in me before pressing kisses along my shoulders and spine. When he withdraws, I fall forward into the mattress. Every part of my body is singing. I feel changed forever. Krane rolls me onto my side next to him, and I taste the salty tears coating my cheeks.

"Scarlett?" His voice is thick with worry. "Did I hurt you? I never should've spoken to you like that. I was too rough, Scar. I'm sorry, I'll never—"

I silence him with a trembling kiss. My body curls into his warm chest, my fingers dance over his birthmark. Everything is right. I would go through all of the pain again to have him like this.

I finally understand his curse.

If what Bram says is true, that he was always going to die, our love was too powerful to let that happen. Death could not separate us. He was brought back to me because we vowed never to be parted. Those words in the *Whispering Woods* had meant something. Our love conquered death, and this was the proof of it.

"You didn't hurt me, Krane. I'm happy—so, so happy."

Relief is stark on his face. I trace the grooves of his pumpkin with my thumb. Krane holds me close, fingers skimming up my spine. Exhaustion weighs me down.

"I'm happy too. Didn't think it would be possible to feel like this again."

Taking a deep breath, I give a solemn nod.

"Tomorrow night, we will go after my father. He has to pay for what he's done."

Krane nods, shifting his fingers through my hair.

"Tomorrow will be a time for vengeance." He presses a kiss to my sweaty brow. "Tonight is a time for love."

I laugh softly, a smile breaking out on my lips.

"Why, Krane, are you saying you love me?"

Biting my lip for dramatic effect, Krane chuckles, pulling me closer.

"You know I do. I love you more than anything."

"I feel the same."

Wrapping his arms around me, sleep beckons. His familiar heartbeat pounds against my ear in the most perfect lullaby. Killing Bram had been easy. For some reason, I can't shake the feeling that my father will put up more of a fight. We will have to be smart to subdue him—it will take both of us.

As long as we have each other, everything will work out as

it's supposed to. I've never been more certain of anything in my life.

18

———

THE HEADLESS HORSEMAN

The sunlight makes her naked skin glow.

In sleep, she looks more like an angel than usual. Her pale lashes fan over her pink cheeks. The meals he's given her have restored her body's softness. He is no longer able to count her ribs—the fullness to her breast and backside makes his mouth water. It was always his dream to see her grow even more, rounder with his child.

It had been a dangerous dream for so many years, and now it feels tangible. Even if he has no idea what a child between them would look like in this new form.

He's getting ahead of himself. He needs to enjoy every moment, not become lost to his greedy desires.

As he looks at her, he realizes just how much he's longed for her. In those dark moments, it was her voice, her face, that called out to him. They strengthened him enough to push through the pain—encouraged him to find her. He thought it was because she was guilty, but that had not been the truth.

He meant what he said. He should've sought her out the moment he was able. Explained to her what happened, and they could've spent the last month together, freely. Instead, he had been warped by anger and the need for revenge. There were still those who needed to pay for his death, but the idea of revenge held less appeal.

Scarlett was his. She was the only thing he ever truly needed. The need for revenge seems so childish compared to their future together. Still, he will breathe easier knowing those who wronged them both are gone from this world.

He will do anything to keep her safe. She has shouldered enough misery for both of them, and that is why he will not allow her to accompany him tonight. The death of her father will not be put upon her shoulders. She may hate the man as much as he does, but that burden may be too great for her to bear. She has suffered enough.

The Headless Horseman will keep her safe even from her own anger. Earl Richard is no fool. Word will have spread of both Bram and the duke's murders, and he will be awaiting him. He will not bring her into that lurking danger. He'll distract her before he slips away.

This ends tonight.

Scarlett stirs against his side. Blinking sleepy blue eyes open at him, he tucks a piece of hair behind her ear. Rose water coats his tongue, accompanying her sweetness that still lingers from the night before. Her smile is serene, making his reanimated heart pump unevenly.

"Good morning," she yawns, stretching out atop the bed.

The sheets slip down her naked body, and she makes no move to cover herself. Her pink nipples harden under his hot stare. His release still coats her thighs. No doubt she'll be sore today after the number of times he took her last night. He couldn't get enough of her—his desire for Scarlett is unending.

"Breakfast?" she asks, her stomach grumbling.

With a sharp nod, he rises from the bed naked. He makes quick work of wrapping her in a blanket before taking her down the hallway. He settles in his same chair from the night before and balances a sleepy Scarlett on his lap. With a wave of his hand, a breakfast feast is revealed. Scarlett gasps, her eyes going wide in delight.

She leans against him while she eats bits of everything, even taking a few pieces from his hand. His fingers dance along her full lower lip, but he does not push until he's certain she's eaten enough. However, he can only help himself for so long.

The blanket slips from her shoulder and bares her breast. Without hesitation, he palms it gently, working her hard nipple —Scarlett moans before playfully smacking at his chest.

"Quit pawing at me while I'm trying to eat."

A laugh booms from deep within him.

"You're moody in the morning."

"I'm ravenous," she says. "A beast ravaged me all night long. I have to keep my strength up in the hopes that he takes me this morning."

Her proud expression sets his blood on fire. His fingers lock around her nipple, gently tugging the stiff peak.

"Is that so?" he asks. "If it is your desire to be taken by such a creature again, then I have the means to make that happen."

"Really?"

She blinks wide us up at him as he tears the blanket from her body. His cock is hard and ready, already leaking moisture. He can smell the delicious scent of her pussy. The soft skin of her inner thighs already glistens with arousal.

Hooking her around her hips, he holds her aloft and fits the head of his cock to her tight entrance. The heat of her pussy makes him hiss.

"Oh, yes."

He lowers her down on his length in one slick glide. Her breath catches as she tosses her head back.

"Too much?"

She shakes her head.

"It's perfect."

Leveraging herself on the arms of the chair, she works herself on his lap. Her ass meets his front in satisfying smacks. He toys with her breasts until she is panting. Her cunt tightens on him like a vice, urging him to spill even if she hasn't hit her peak yet.

Her movements become halting, her rhythm becoming disjointed in the face of her pleasure. He takes over, powering up from beneath her and shoving himself deep. Broken moans fall from her red lips as she tosses her head back against his shoulder. His fingers find her greedy clit and rub tight circles on it.

A breath catches in her throat, and she erupts, clenching down on him and encouraging him to spear deep inside of her and empty himself in a rush of hot seed. He fills her to the brim, delighting in how it seeps from her tight hole and coats both of them.

She pants as he holds her close, memorizing the beat of her heart—taking it with him. Scarlett will no doubt be mad once she realizes what he's done. He can take her ire; what he couldn't withstand was her being hurt. If she can be mad at him, it means she is alive, and he will just work even harder to secure her forgiveness again.

Capturing her face, he trails his fingers along her cheek.

"I love you. I'll always protect you, Scarlett." His eyes harden, and her lips part. "Even from yourself."

Her pale brows lower in confusion.

"Please forgive me for this."

Before she can open her mouth and ask his intention, he waves his hand. Deep sleep settles over her, and she drops into his lap. He can only pray that by the time she wakes, he has returned to her, leaving her father's corpse rotting inside their manor.

19

—————

SCARLETT

Something is very, very wrong.

I feel it the moment my eyes open. Not only because it's dark in my room when the last memory I have is of morning breakfast with Krane. No, what concerns me the most is that I am alone. Where is Krane? I sit up quickly and swing my legs over. The next indication that something is off is the soreness.

Or the lack thereof.

I'm used to the aftereffects of Krane's vigorous lovemaking. I should be feeling tender at the very least, thanks to his new endowments. There is some slight discomfort, but nothing out of the ordinary. My muscles feel like they've been asleep for a long time, waking with pins and needles.

Unease grips me. I have to find Krane. Now.

Dressing quickly, I head out of my room, calling his name. It is deadly quiet inside the castle. I can hear every groan and shift of the crumbling structure. I open every door upstairs as I shuffle through my last memory.

He had asked me to forgive him. Forgive him for what? My mouth feels full of poison. Krane is nowhere to be found.

He had asked me to forgive him, and then nothing. I couldn't remember anything after that—everything had gone dark, just like when he took me from my wedding day. The puzzle pieces come together in my mind. Krane put me to sleep, but why? How long have I been out for?

Pushing into the dining room, our breakfast feast still lies atop the table. My stomach sinks as I take in the state of the food. A day left unattended would not cause this. The bread has molded around the edges. The fat on the bacon has solidified and is turning black. The eggs are drier than dust. One ripe, ruby apple remains in the fruit basket. A single worm tunnels through the rotten flesh, exposing the mealy inside.

I swallow down my vomit, quickly turning from the room.

I have to get out of here. I have to find Krane; something terrible has happened. I can feel it. I exit the front of the castle, still calling for him even though I know it is of no use. He wouldn't intentionally abandon me. If he put me to sleep, he thought he was coming back. So why hasn't he?

Mounted out in front is his horse. I approached the creature cautiously. Holding up my hands, I take a deep breath.

"Do you know where he's gone?"

I don't know if the animal can understand me, but I have to try. Much to my surprise, the horse flicks its head as if it's nodding—a deep fog rolls in from the woods, blanketing the ground. I disregard the chill and use all my strength to mount the towering horse.

Taking the reins in my hands, I urge the beast forward, and it launches into a gallop. The wind whips at my hair and tugs at my gown. I have no idea where we are going.

The only thing I can hope for is that Krane is still there and I'm too late to save him.

THE HEADLESS HORSEMAN

He was a fool.

A no-good, stubborn, headstrong fool. He had once asked Scarlett why she hadn't left with him, and she had said she was scared and wanted time to plan a way to ensure their safety. She had admitted they should've just left, and that's exactly what he should've done as well.

Revenge was not worth this. Coming back here was not worth it.

He could only hope now that she would be safe. If she learned of what happened to him, he prayed she would not come searching. He hopes his magic will keep her asleep until this is over. He will use his last breath to beg for them to be reunited in death if his were ever to be granted.

The silver shackles around his wrist have weakened him considerably. He doesn't know where her father got them from. If only he hadn't acted so rashly. He should've come up with a better plan than an ambush. Earl Richard Crest had been expecting that and easily slapped the shackles on him whilst he was busy dispatching some of the earl's guards.

Freshly torn skin knits back together along his back. The

crumbling remnants of his pumpkin make it hard to see. A sharp squeal of hinges echoes down into the dungeon, making his breath turn ragged.

Pain always follows that sound.

Heavy footsteps descend the stairs until the sconces illuminate Scarlett's father. They look nothing alike. She had always favored her mother. It is shocking that a man as cruel as him sired someone as wonderful as Scarlett.

The stone hearth has dwindled considerably. The earl whistles as he stokes the flame into a roaring orange inferno. The wooden bench below him is caked with his dark blood. He has been shackled to it for hours each day. The only reprieve will come later, when Earl Richard grows bored and tosses his bleeding, broken body into one of the cells.

Through one hazy eye hole, he can make out the earl jamming a poker into the fire. His own green flames have been diminished, barely more than a kindling. The metal glows orange as the earl turns. Running a hand through his short beard, the man looks thoughtful.

A wicked gleam dances in his dark eyes.

"Your skin regrows when I cut it off. Now let's see how it fares being burned."

The earl's steps grow closer, and the Headless Horseman tries to blank his mind. To go into that dark place he clung to during his transformation. Scarlett's lovely face swirls in his mind. Her floral scent, the feel of her soft lips, the way his name sounds moaned in his ear, how tight her—

Her memory evaporates when the hot poker presses against his exposed flesh. A scream rips from his lungs. He can feel it sizzle and bubble. Again and again it is applied as the earl callously laughs. The scent of burning flesh is heavy in the air.

"Scream all you want. We've only just begun."

He is going to die down here.

21

SCARLETT

Crow's Claw Manor looks just the same.

That is, except for the dozens of king's guards patrolling the lawn. Pressing myself further against a sturdy oak tree, I make sure the shadow conceals me completely. A heavy fog rolls in from the forest, further hiding me from the guard's watchful eyes. I keep my eyes locked on each patrol, waiting for an opening.

Krane is here. I can feel it in my bones. The moment his horse came to a halt at the edge of my father's land, I knew something terrible had befallen him. Why would he come alone? A more disheartening question is, what has delayed him this long? My heart squeezes painfully in my chest at the thought of him in pain.

He has already suffered enough.

Voices float along the wind, growing louder. Flattening myself against the base of the tree, I hold my breath, not daring to move. The rattling of armor steals my attention up the path. Two soldiers come into view armed to the teeth. They glance towards me, but see nothing in the thick fog.

Both unstrap their sword belts and toss them atop a crim-bling statue before pulling down their trousers and beginning to piss. Both blissfully unaware of my presence, I don't make a sound. The taller one on the left with a scar running along his cheek stretches his neck back.

"What do you think the earl is doing with that *thing*?" he asks.

The other one merely shrugs, concentrating on his own bodily functions.

"No idea. The only thing I know is he paid a sorceress a small fortune for those shackles to bind him." The shorter guard huffs a laugh. "Keeps that creature as weak as a babe."

"I couldn't believe it when I saw it. A pumpkin for a head?" The taller man huffs a laugh. "That headless horseman story is just an old wives' tale."

"Clearly not."

My heart pounds unevenly in my chest. I place a hand over my mouth to keep from crying out. Krane is here—captured— and at the mercy of my father. I have to get to him, but I have to be smart about it. While my heart urges me into action, my brain tells me to calm down and think rationally. If I get captured, I will be in no position to save him.

Both men retie their trousers but make no move to return to their patrol. They cross their arms over their massive chests. My eyes land on their discarded weapons. Clinging to the mist, I travel on silent feet until they are only a few feet away. I'll have to break from the treeline and not falter if I wish to remain unseen.

"Whatever Earl Richard is doing to that thing, it won't stop screaming. I can hear its fucking wails all the way inside my tent." Each word drips with disgust. "How long are we meant to remain stationed here?"

With both men's focus on each other, I sink into the tall, damp grass. My gown clings to me as I crawl towards their weapons. The breeze whips above me, hopefully concealing any sounds I'm making. The weapons are just in view when a voice rises above the wind.

"The king has tasked us with keeping him safe. With Duke Marc and his son dead, the king has ordered Earl Richard to be elevated to Duke of Broken Cliff. We are to keep him safe until the royal decree arrives."

Taking a steady breath, I grip the handle of the nearest dagger—the smooth hilt glides against my palm. I unsheath it slowly, the silver blade glinting in the moonlight. I hold it to my chest, glancing over my shoulder, expecting to be discovered. The two guards are still locked in conversation, their bodies drifting closer to the woods.

Glancing back, I see the crumbling remnants of the statue below. A fist-sized piece of marble catches my eye. Lifting it into my palm, I act before I can think better of it. Hurtling it into the dark, the stone echoes off the trunks of several trees before landing with a thud deep inside the woods.

"What was that?" one of the guards snaps.

"No idea, let's—"

I don't stick around to hear the rest of their conversation. Rising on trembling knees, I lift my skirts and take off in a sprint. The night wind tongue at me as my destination looms above. No one is better at sneaking into this home unseen than I. I watched the patrols long enough to gauge when one would overlap with the other.

A brief window presented itself, enough for me to crest the hill and slip in through the side unseen. The familiar brick alcove looms, and I throw myself against it. Panting silently, I collapse behind an old, worn barrel and wait. A handful of seconds later, the sound of clanking armor rattles towards me, the second half of the patrol making their rounds.

No cry of alarm is raised. I've made it nearly there unseen. I thank my lucky stars as I wait for the king's guards to pass. My mind wanders to Krane. I brace myself for the condition I'll find him in. With him weakened by whatever shackles my father procured, I can only imagine the torture he's endured.

With the guards out of earshot, I prowl along the side of the house and quickly unlatch the kitchen door. I hold it until it gently shuts, praying for the hinges to remain silent. Once it is closed and latched, and I hear no sound of approaching guards, I take a breath. Turning into the dark room, the kitchen is bare.

No loaves of fresh bread have been left to cool on the counters. The shelves and cupboards look empty, save for a singular bottle of brandy. It is eerily quiet, making the manor feel more like a tomb than ever. I no longer fear the ghosts that once called this manor home.

There are worse evils to fear here than those of phantoms.

My stomach sinks as I walk along the stone floor. If Krane is here, there is only one place my father is keeping him. The dungeon was never used when I was growing up here. The rusted iron hinges of the door leading deep into the bowels of Crow's Claw Manor are a testament to how rarely this room was opened.

I swallow, my trembling hands pulling on the chain. The door groans open. The loud echo cannot be helped. I need to move fast if I want to get Krane out of here. I say a silent prayer that I'm not walking into a trap set by my father.

The wooden stairs are quiet against my slippered feet. Gripping the handle, I glide down them quickly. The scent of death nearly chokes me. Dank and rot permeate the air the deeper I go. Once at the bottom, I can make out a roaring fireplace.

Orange flames lick along the stone mantle. In the center of the room, metal chains hang from the ceiling. There is a row of cells along the far wall, too dark inside for me to make anything out. A wooden bench is coated in all manner of grime and dark blood. Deadly sharp blades and a still steaming poke rest beside it. Vomit swims up my throat, but I choke it back down. I feel light-headed. Bracing my hand against the stone wall, I try to get my bearings as best I can.

A sharp, ragged wheezing echoes from the middle cell. I hurry over to it, lighting the torch beside it as quickly as I can.

"Krane," I call into the darkness.

I can only see the glistening tips of his leather boots.

"Krane," I repeat. "It's me."

His harsh breath catches, as his feet twitch slightly. He folds them away, and I hold my breath. Nothing could have prepared me for what I see next. It is almost as devastating as the day I found his corpse in the woods.

His pumpkin head has been smashed in along the sides. Deep gauges have been carved along each side, forming a crude design. He trembles beneath a scratchy, wool blanket. Sweat gleams along his gray skin. Large gashes run along his shoulders and neck. The raised and bubbled skin along his chest is new. The green fire inside his eyes is dim. It flickers weakly as it takes me in.

Around his pale wrists are delicate silver shackles, engraved with some sort of writing.

"Scarlett," he wheezes.

His trembling hand lifts through the bars, and I lower myself to meet it. Fingers graze over my cheek as tears beckon. A green flame flickers to life before dying with a hiss.

"Am I dreaming?"

My laugh is watery as I capture his hand with my palm.

"No, I am here, my love. Come to free you."

Krane pulls back, his skin somehow turning more pale. He thrashes his head side to side, moaning sharply.

"It's too dangerous. You shouldn't be here."

The dagger in my hand suddenly feels useless. How am I going to free him from those metal bindings? More importantly, how am I going to free him from behind these bars? Maybe he knows where the key is.

"How long have you been down here? How can I get you out?" I ask.

Krane's body begins to tremble violently.

"I don't know. Most likely a week."

That makes me come up short.

"I was asleep for a week?"

Even with his dying flames, he manages to look sheepish.

"I'm sorry, Scar. I thought I was doing the right thing—sparing you from the burden of killing your father." His laugh holds no humor. "Now I realize that my revenge made me foolish. In my greed to punish him, I lost everything. Go now, save yourself. With these shackles, I am as good as dead."

I shake my head, my eyes narrowing. The thought of leaving him behind is unimaginable. If he is to die, then we will die together. We vowed never to be apart, and not even death can separate us.

"I'm not leaving you. I love you. I'll find a way to free you from this."

"How touching," a sneering voice booms behind me.

I launch to my feet. Whipping around, my back presses against the cold bars of Krane's cell. My father is there, wickedness dancing in his dark eyes. There is a madness there I haven't seen before. Standing at his side is my mother. Her blue eyes glaze over, not daring to meet my own.

Anger flows hotly through my veins. This is the man who killed my beloved Krane. The man who stole my future and even now delights in the fiendish torture he's inflicting on my love. I bare my teeth at him and extend my dagger. I will not go down without a fight.

"Release him," I command, straightening my spine. "Release him and we will spare your life."

My father laughs loudly, nearly doubling over. A flicker of awareness kindles in my mother's eyes, but it quickly vanishes.

His vile amusement only makes my anger grow. His callousness cost me everything.

"You are in no position to make demands of me." He wipes his eyes. "Ungrateful, brat. You could've been a duchess—lived in luxury after supplying Bram with a few heirs. You gave it all up for that *thing.*"

He waves a dismissive hand at Krane.

"This ends tonight. Once that creature is dead, I will find another lord to marry you off to. I don't care if the marriage has to be consummated with a knife to your throat. You will do as I tell you."

A scream tears from my lungs. All the pent-up rage I've felt over the years is bubbling to the surface. Nothing was ever good enough for him. No matter how hard I tried to be perfect or obey his rules, thinking it would allow me my freedom, it never mattered. He didn't care that I loved Krane—that even if we had no money, we would be wealthier than my father could imagine because we had love.

My father never loved me—neither did my mother. They only saw me as a way to increase their power—my mother saw me as a doll she could play with until that doll started forming her own opinions. I had wasted years of my life playing by their rules, and it had cost me everything. Now, I am done. It was time to settle this on my terms.

My father's eyes widen as I charge at him with the dagger extended. I slice at his silk shirt, but he manages to dodge any deadly blows. Subduing my wrists, he throws the dagger away. Squeezing my bones to the point of breaking, he looks over his shoulder.

"Guards!" he barks.

Two sets of heavy footsteps pound down the stairs. The king's guards are dressed in their white armour, the royal crest decorating their chest plates. My father swiftly hands my shrieking form over to them. I buck and thrash against their grips, trying my best to break free.

"Listen here," my father snarls. "You can watch as I kill your bastard lover. Again."

I bare my teeth at him, shaking with fury. The scent of burning wood wraps around me. I need to be smart, but my rage is too great. My body's only instinct is to fight until the bitter end.

"This time, it will be permanent," my father declares.

With a sharp nod, one of the guards releases me. My arms are pinned behind my back as the other goes to Krane's cell and unlocks it. A sob rattles me as Krane is pulled free. In the stark light, the pain he's been subjected to is even more gruesome. The skin of his back has been flayed and burned. The gray edges curl up along the sides of the wounds. Muscles have been sliced back until pale white bone pokes free.

The state of his hands reveals missing fingers cut down to bloody stubs. My stomach rolls and I nearly choke on bile.

"No!" I scream, my wild eyes searching for any way out of this. "Mother! Stop this. Do something!"

My mother looks up, her face once the woman I turned to for comfort. There is a warmth there that I remember, but the frigid mask of Countess Christina quickly wipes it. She is not my mother; she is Earl Richard Crest's wife.

"I'm sorry, Scarlett." Her voice is flat. "There is nothing that can be done now."

"Silence," my father commands. "This thing doesn't seem to die no matter how much pain it's in—how much blood it loses."

The guard drops Krane's arm, and he nearly falls to the floor. His green fire is barely an ember now. He could heal from these wounds, but not with those shackles weakening him. If only I could've removed them, we might've had a fighting chance.

"The priest who meant to marry you and Earl Bram had come to me a week ago, telling me of the creature who had slaughtered the duke. I was sure he was mistaken—sure no such thing existed, but just in case, I found a sorceress who could aid me for a steep price. Once Earl Bram was found dead, I knew it was a matter of time before that thing came for me." My father chuckles, digging into his coat pocket. "She had informed me that the Headless Horseman is a vengeful spirit—forged from a restless soul murdered unjustly. I could only think of one person who that could be, and I knew this would only end in death. His or mine. She told me they were near impossible to kill. Unless I had this."

Ice coats my veins as my father produces a small pistol from his pocket. The barrel is engraved with the same markings etched into Krane's shackles. It glints in the low light of the dungeon. My father's smile widens into deadly points. His polluted soul rises to the surface.

"Cost nearly my weight in gold," my father proclaims proudly.

Of that, I have no doubt, that kind of weapon comes from far-off lands. The king would have his head if he learned my father was in possession of one. Producing a silver bullet, he loads it into the chamber. His meaty thumb digs into the hammer, pulling it back until the distinct click of a bullet rattles into position.

"One shot should do the trick."

Krane doesn't even try to flee. He's too weak. It's a miracle he's still standing upright. Gore and blood are dried along his chest and stain the top of his pants. Green flames flicker for a moment as he lifts his head towards me—my vision blurs with unshed tears.

He's not strong enough to speak, but I hear his words echo down our bond. They whisper into my heart and solidify in my soul. He's giving me his love, beseeching me to forgive him. I can almost hear his frantic plea. He wishes we had more time

—that every moment together was a precious gift. Wherever we go in death, he'll be waiting for me. Our love is eternal.

My father levels the gun at Krane's chest.

A cry builds in my throat. All of my love and anger fuel me, strengthen me in a way I haven't felt before. This can't be the end. We haven't endured all this pain not to get our happy ending. My shriek surprises the guard enough to loosen his grip just enough for me to yank myself free.

Without time to think, I rush towards Krane. His green flames expand, but I'm moving too fast for him to stop me. I launch myself in front of him, soaring through the air just in time to watch my father squeeze the trigger. A loud bang assaults my ears. Blooming pain erupts in my abdomen.

I gasp, clattering against Krane. He manages to lift his hands and cradle me to him. Looking down, crimson liquid pools along the front of my gown. I press a hand there, sticky blood soaking it instantly.

"Foolish child," my father spits behind me.

Krane collapses to his knees, holding me tightly against him. I wanted to die for so long, and now with the certainty of it looming, I feel a strange sense of peace. Perhaps because he is here, holding me to him. I won't be alone in my final moments. The pain is shocking, nearly stealing my vision.

Lifting my blood-soaked hand, I cup his crumbling cheek. The flames dance inside his eyes, trying to ignite and failing. My tongue turns heavy in my mouth, but I press on.

"I love you," I whisper.

Krane whimpers, his mutilated fingers digging into me.

"You are my sun. I am your moon. We will be reunited again. Nothing can ever keep us apart."

"Scarlett," he rasps.

Inside his pumpkin, a green flame kindles, sparks, and holds steady.

From that one flame, an inferno is born. With a shattering

growl, the room around me erupts into emerald fire. It licks over every surface, melting the shackles along the ceiling and the bars of the cells. Guards scream, my father yells at my mother to run, but it's too late. Flames engulf them all. My eyes can barely see a thing, only fuzzy shapes and soft edges.

The silver of his shackles melts away, hitting the floor with a hiss. Krane rises, his skin threading back together before my eyes. His pumpkin glows, restored. I think I say his name. He looks at me as if I did, but it's all too hazy.

The last thing I remember is a wall of green before the darkness claims me.

22

THE HEADLESS HORSEMAN

He carries her limp body from the horse.

Luminous pale skin has turned ashen. Scarlett's full ruby lips are blue, and her chest weakly shudders up and down. Death hangs heavy in the air tonight. Each body he passed on the way out of the manor had erupted in green fire. He was never more powerful than he was right now, and yet none of it mattered.

If he could not save her, then what was the point?

He cannot lose her, not now. After just finding her, the blood soaking the front of her gown seeks to take her away. In death, he cannot follow. Not as he is now. He has to find some way to save her. He'll barter with his soul for the chance to heal her. Life means nothing if she isn't here beside him.

The forest curls around them like fingers. Fog forms a thick blanket along the ground, covering him up to his ankles. The Headless Horseman has no idea where he's taking her. Some invisible sting pulls him deeper into the *Whispering Woods.* Closer to the place where he met his own end.

Whatever magic spared him that night could do the same for her. Even if she were cursed, they would still be together, toiling away as two monsters until the end of time. It would be enough just to have her, even if he wished he could spare her from the pain of the transformation.

His boots slow in the dirt. Gently, he sets her down amongst the mist. The thick fog encases her like a death shroud. Her skin is far too pale, and her chest…he swallows. Her chest has gone still. A broken sob leaves him, and he falls forward.

The soft swells of her breast cushion his pumpkin head as he cries against her. Her face is serene in death. Her blood wets him, and her heart remains quiet. With a shuddering breath, he appeals to the moon. Beseeches it to spare her from this untimely fate. Screaming, weeping, and praying, the forest is filled with the sounds of his despair.

His whole body freezes as something brushes along his shoulder. Glancing up, he sees nothing, though the imprint of phantom fingers remains on his skin. The fog grows thicker, nearly swallowing her whole.

"Krane," a voice echoes from the fog. "*Krane.*"

The mist swirls around him. Shadows dance on every corner. His eyes are wild as she searches through the darkness, trying to find that soft voice calling out to him. Spinning around, he gasps at the sight before him.

Scarlett. Alive.

Her cheeks are pink. Mischief sparks in her blue eyes. Her teeth sink into her full lower lip as she flutters her lashes at him. How is this possible? Is this a dream? A figment of his imagination?

"What are you doing out here? You should know better than to venture into the *Whispering Woods*."

Glancing down, her corpse is gone. Only this vision of her remains, looking at him expectantly. Apprehension tears at his stomach, but he doesn't try to flee. Something urges him to stay. The feel of her soul against his encourages him to remain in place.

Her warmth flows from her. The soft scent of rose water makes his mouth water as she drifts closer. Something flickers in her eyes as her grin grows.

"Were you hoping to get me alone? Somewhere no one could find us?"

Her teasing tone causes his cock to twitch. She is his siren, luring him to her with barely a smile. Her fingers drift over his pumpkin, as if she has done it a thousand times before. This vision of her knows him as he is now. Whatever this is, he must see it through to the end..

Finding his voice, he manages a nod.

"Yes."

His voice is rough. Scarlett giggles, reaching behind herself and making quick work of the lace of her gown. It falls into the fog, leaving her gloriously naked. Her pink nipples pebble in the moonlight. A dusting of golden hair conceals her intimate flesh. He can smell her arousal, and his mouth waters in anticipation of a taste.

"If you wanted me that badly, we needn't go this far into the woods," she purrs.

Her hands fall to his shoulders, and she pushes him back. Her supple body falls atop his hard one. Groaning at the feel of her, his hands find her backside, gently kneading each firm cheek. Scarlett sighs, her eyes turning heavy.

"Again? You just had me."

His cock kicks to life between them, and she rubs against it. Her mewls of pleasure spur him on, holding her tighter to him.

"I'll never have enough." The words are growled against her lips. "I could spend every day buried inside you, and it still wouldn't be enough."

She pulls up, the fog spreading behind her like wings. It curls heavily around her glorious breasts. Her nipples are begging for his tongue. She mewls, rubbing her cunt against his seeking hardness. She feels solid—permanent.

"You and that filthy mouth," she sighs. "Put it to use, Krane."

Their mouths come together in a searing kiss. In one fluid motion, he rolls her beneath him. The fog envelopes her, making her glow like the moon. His moon, forever.

He spares her nipples a few licks before descending towards her center. The smooth skin of her thighs grazes along his pumpkin. Hooking her legs over his shoulders, he pushes her back and exposes her pink flesh to his gaze. Her greedy clit begs for his attention. Her tight cunt begs him to fill it.

The first taste of her jolts a torrent of seed from his cock. It coats the inside of his trousers, making them sticky. He pays it no mind, only delights in her sweet, musky flavor. Scarlett arches her back, thrusting her tits towards the sky. His hand reaches up to palm one of her breasts as the other spears inside her entrance.

Wet heat envelopes his hand as he pumps two fingers into her. He feels her begin to clench down on him, and his lips latch onto her clit. She screams her release, bucking wildly against him as he licks up her spend. Without hesitation, he shucks his trousers and enters her with one harsh thrust.

He captures her groan in his mouth. Whatever final kindness is allowing him to have her this way, he will not question. Perhaps they both died in her father's dungeon, and this is what death is. He would be grateful for it. He needs nothing beyond her. Ever.

"Faster, my love. Claim me."

Her mewls of pleasure spur him on. Pulling himself from her wetness, he deftly flips her onto her front. She moans as he smacks the pale globe of her ass and watches the color bloom on her fair skin. Taking hold of her hips, he reenters her quickly. A pounding rhythm is set as her fingers dig into the ground below them.

Scarlett begins to tighten on him. The delicate muscles of her pussy clench down on his thrusting cock. It hardens inside her, and he needs more. Pulling her back, he fits her snuggly to her lap and powers into her from below. Her breasts bounce with the force of his thrusts.

His hand cups her throat, feeling every whimper against his palm.

"I'm close," she says, teeth sinking into her lip. "I wish we could stay like this forever."

He pounds into her with a punishing rhythm.

"We can," he vows. "Whatever you want, I'll give it to you."

Scarlett gasps as his hand finds her clit. He works it as she rises and falls in his lap. Her tight pussy grips him like a fist. Inside of her is blissful torture—the edge between heaven and hell.

"You can save me, Krane," she moans. "Relinquish the rage —the revenge. Give in to your love for me. I will be yours again just as you are mine."

She sinks down on him with finality. Her words ring in his head as she comes with a cry of his name. Bliss erupts within him, and he thrusts deep inside her, emptying himself with a vow.

"I give it all back. My need for revenge has been satisfied. Nothing matters if I don't have you, my moon. Take whatever you need from me to repair yourself. Every part of me has always been yours from the moment we met."

She looks at him, tears shining in her eyes. Fog rolls in, blanketing everything, and then she is gone as if she had never been there at all.

23

———

SCARLETT

The first thing I see is the overlapping branches above me.

Then I feel it. The rise and fall of my chest, my blood-soaked gown sticking to my skin. I feel along my abdomen, but there is no hole. Nothing but unblemished skin greets my fingers. I gasp, sitting up, and something heavy slips off my side.

A disgruntled groan follows.

I can hardly believe what I'm seeing. Floppy, reddish-brown hair falls heavily over his smooth brow. His tan skin is pink and freckled. It can't be—how?

"Krane," I gasp.

His only response is to moan, throwing an arm over his eyes. No longer holes in a pumpkin, his large eyes and full mouth sit proportionate on his face. The sharpness of his jaw is covered by a short beard beginning to grow.

"It's too early," he grumbles, before lowering his arm.

I was wrong. He's not exactly how he was. Krane is taller—the same height he was as the Headless Horseman, and with the same impressive build. His ears are sharper than those of a human man. When he finally blinks his sleepy eyes open at me, I can't suppress my gasp.

Green flames comprise his irises. They snap and dance around his dark pupil. It is a breathtaking sight. His lips tug into a grin as he stretches out beside me on the grass.

"Well, good morning to you, too." Rising into a sitting position, he shakes his head. "I had the strangest dream."

"Krane."

"Somehow, I had a pumpkin for a head. We shouldn't sneak wine from your father's cellar anymore, Scar."

"Krane," I snap. "That wasn't a dream."

His dark brows lower.

"What are you talking about? Of course it was—"

He pauses. With widening eyes, he looks at me, really looks at me. He takes me in from head to toe, eyes lingering on the front of my gown—the crimson stain unmistakable in the morning sun. With a gasp, he looks at his hands. His long fingers end in short nails with freckles along his knuckles. He takes stock of himself, patting his chest and face. Raking a hand through his hair, the flames in his eyes blaze.

Removing his coat, he holds up one of the sparkling buttons to get a better look. Shaking his head, he grips the garment in his fingers.

"I'm me again," he whispers hoarsely.

"Almost. The eyes are a bit strange." I pause. "As are your sharp fangs and pointed ears."

"Beats a pumpkin head," Krane says. "How can this be?"

There is a predatory grace to his movements. The primal edge he had remains. He is human—and yet not.

"I don't know," I say honestly.

His eyes drift to the stain on my gown. Reaching towards me, he gently presses a warm palm to my abdomen. With a shuddering breath, he meets my eyes.

"I watched you die, Scarlett. How are you here, too?"

"Maybe we're in heaven," I suggest.

Seems like a logical enough answer.

"I'm not so sure about that." Rising onto his long legs, he reaches down to help me to my feet. "Only one way to find out."

We make the short journey back towards Crow's Claw Manor. The sight of a smoldering home collapsing in on itself is all the confirmation we both need. We aren't in heaven. That horrible house would be in neither one of ours.

I glance up at him, pink spreading along his cheeks.

"When you got shot, I lost it. My power consumed me and eradicated everyone inside the house." Green flames spark from his palms at the memory. "Well, that's something."

I hear his words for what they are. There are no survivors. My parents are both dead, and I don't have it in me to grieve. We were not a loving family—they would've trapped me in a horrible marriage and denied me my one true happiness. May they rot where they lie.

"Where should we go now?" I ask, the wind tugging at my hair.

The sun shines from behind the dense clouds. The first sunny day in over a month makes goosebumps erupt on my flesh. Krane plays with his green flames, letting them dance between his fingers. Twisting his lips, he waves his hand, and my ruined gown is replaced with a pale pink frock. He does the same to his own clothes, transforming them into a simple satin shirt and pants. A thick cloak drapes around his shoulders.

"Back to Nightingale Castle?" he suggests.

A mischievous smile curves his lips as he hooks an arm around my waist. I go to him willingly, a long-overdue homecoming. He's even taller than me now. I have to crane my neck back to meet his gaze. The feel of his heartbeat echoes my own.

"I want to celebrate your return to life the best way I know how." His lips find my ear. "Want to put my new tongue to use on your sweet cunt."

A giggle escapes me.

"What an offer. How could any girl possibly refuse such a declaration?"

He kisses along my cheek, his hand drifting down my back.

"We could always fuck in the barn one final time? Give that place a proper send-off."

"Hmm," I hum low in my throat as his mouth explores my neck. "I don't have a particular fondness for combing hay out of my hair later."

He nips my ear, making me turn slippery between my thighs.

"What if I promise to—"

The sound of thunderous footsteps makes us both pull back.

Dust flies along the loan road as a large carriage flanked by several armed riders approaches. The king's crest is emblazoned on the door. I glance towards Krane; from a distance, he looks human. Enough that he shouldn't raise too many questions, but he should still keep his distance from whoever is approaching. The horses halt a few feet away from us. A page comes to open the door, but it flies open before he can reach his post.

King Herbert descends the short steps dressed in golden robes that perfectly complement his sparkling crown. He casts a long glance at us before I yank Krane's arm and we both sink into bows.

"Your majesty," we say in unison.

Fear grips me. If he has discovered what we've done, or who we are, there could be trouble. We need to play this smart. The king turns a watchful eye on us. The wrinkles around his eyes and mouth deepen as he frowns.

"What has occurred here?"

I swallow, glancing towards Krane. He answers before I can.

"A fire, sir. It claimed everyone inside."

The king takes a step closer, eyes narrowing.

"And who might you be?"

Krane opens his mouth, but no words come out. Thinking quickly, I fall back on all my training as an earl's daughter. My nobility may be the only thing that gets us out of this alive. Hope threads through me; this is our chance to have the future I wanted for us. To spit in the face of my father's legacy and claim it for ourselves.

"Lady Scarlett Crest, your majesty," I say softly. "This is my husband, Lord Krane Crest."

I can feel Krane stiffen beside me, a silent understanding passing between us. We have one shot at this, and both of us need to be convincing in our roles. Shouldn't be too hard, as it's not even really a lie. I have the scar to prove it.

The king drags a hand through his long, white beard.

"Weren't you the one sent to marry Earl Bram?"

I swallow, willing my eyes to turn sad.

"Yes, until he was killed. Then I was taken by a horrible creature deep into the woods." I take Krane's hand in mine, squeezing it gently. "That is where Krane found me. Rescued me from that foul creature and brought me back home. My father believed the only way to repay his kindness was to wed him to me and name Krane his heir. We only said our vows last night and were away to consummate our marriage."

The king considers my words. It is a believable enough story, but the king is no fool. After a moment, he takes another step towards us until he is only a few feet away.

"And do you have proof from your father of such declarations? You will have to forgive me, but I can't just take your words as true."

I swallow a curse as my mind comes up short trying to think of anything that would persuade him. Krane drops my hand, and I turn towards him. From his pocket, he produces a piece of parchment stamped with my father's official seal.

"It is here, your majesty."

Never have I been more grateful for Krane's magic than I am right now.

The king takes the offered parchment between his bony fingers. His eyes drift over the seal before he snaps the wax. Unfolding the paper, his eyes take in each line of the page. Wide, brown eyes look up at us.

"Earl Richard Crest has named you his heir and successor. By marrying his daughter, you will take on the Crest name. His money and holdings will now become yours upon his death." The king tucks the parchment into his robes. "Well, a bit of bad luck, as your family home now sits in ruin. If you need a place to stay while it's being rebuilt, Darkwood Castle sits empty. I was on my way here to name your father Duke of Broken Cliff, but now that title falls to you, Duke Krane."

My heart lifts as I look at Krane. It has all worked out in the end. My lord husband was someone I loved. We would've been happy with nothing, but there is satisfaction in knowing the legacy my father sold me off to preserve will now be ours. Our children will never know their grandfather. The Crest family will start anew, with its foundation in love, not ambition.

"We won't let you down, sire."

Krane bows to the king, and I follow suit.

"See that you don't." He gestures towards the large chest attached to the back of his carriage. "I'll take the gold I had intended for your father to Darkwood Castle. I'm assuming his treasury survived the blaze."

"Yes, your majesty. He never kept his valuables in the main house," I confirm.

Krane raises a brow at me as the king merely nods. Turning around, he returns to his carriage.

"Very good. I hope you two enjoy your new marriage. Condolences for your losses." His eyes turn sharp over his shoulders. "I'd work on looking a bit sadder if I were you. Wouldn't want anyone thinking this wasn't an accident."

Heat sweeps up my cheeks as Krane and I extend another bow towards him. We stay silent as his carriage turns around and hurries down the gravel path. We watch it until it becomes a speck on the horizon. I turn towards Krane, happiness nearly making me buoyant.

"You're a wonderful liar," he compliments.

"I was taught by the best." I go into his arms, allowing him to hold me close. "Duke Krane has a nice ring to it."

He chuckles, his deep voice making my body come alive.

"As does Duchess Scarlett."

I nod at him. We will have our parts to play. We would be fools to think we were entirely out of the woods yet, but this is a significant step forward. Part of me is still reeling from every-thing that's happened.

"I can't believe it," I whisper. "Despite the odds, I've somehow gotten almost everything I've ever wanted."

Krane's brows lower.

"What more could you possibly want?"

I lick my lips before smiling up at him.

"I can think of one thing."

If he catches my meaning, he doesn't let on, but nor does he stop me from pulling him after me. It doesn't take long for us to reach the old wooden doors of the barn. The structure is untouched. Unlatching the door, the familiar groan of the hinges greets us. I turn towards a smiling Krane, whose hands along my back are already leading me into the stables.

"I thought you didn't want hay in your hair."

"That was before I found out I'd be fucking a duke," I sigh, reaching for his shirt and tossing it aside. "One last time. A proper goodbye to this place."

My hands trail up the contours of his stomach. The warm muscles tickle my palms, sending a hot need coursing through me. Krane backs me up, waving a hand and spreading his cloak atop a pile of hay bales. Together, we quickly shed both of our clothes, our naked skin slides together as sunlight streams down from the ceiling slats.

Krane falls between my open thighs, groaning as my pussy rubs against his cock. The rigids remain, and I'm grateful for his transformation all over again. The familiar scent of hay and dust wraps around us. I kiss the heart on his shoulder and stare up into his flaming eyes.

Love pours from his gaze and into my heart.

We don't have to be quiet. Not as he devours my pussy with the broadside of his tongue or when he pushes all the way inside me on one thrust. Our bodies slap together, and our moans rise towards the sky. Our kisses are frantic as if making up for lost time, and then slower, realizing that we have all the time in the world now.

I had been lost without him. A wraith that floated around, longing to join her love beyond the grave. I had loved him as a poor stable boy, as the Headless Horseman of Broken Cliff, and now as a duke. No matter what he looked like—no matter where he went—he would always be mine. Our souls had become one from the moment we met, and we would fight for each other with every breath.

It wasn't always easy, but it was worth it. To have him now, deep inside of me, reaffirming his love with each hard thrust, makes all the painful days without him disappear. We had our whole future ahead of us. The shackles of the past had been cast aside. There was no need for revenge when our future was so bright.

There was only space for love now. The rage was gone.

Only one thing remained for us to have, but that shouldn't take too long to accomplish. In fact, it could have already happened, or maybe it's happening right now. The thought sends me headlong into my climax, and it spurs Krane to spill himself deep inside me with a groan of my name against my lips.

I smile, knowing my final wish is now even closer than before.

Krane kisses my sweaty brow and holds me close. We will enjoy each other again once we catch our breath. His fingers shift through my hair just like he always does. Our racing heartbeats twin together.

"I love you, Scarlett."

I smile against his birthmark.

"I love you more."

EPILOGUE

KRANE - ONE YEAR LATER

My wife is as beautiful as ever.

Every year, I watched her grow more and more lovely. It seems impossible, yet after another year together, I can say that her beauty will never wane. She is kind and compassionate to the people of our land. She is a wicked and tempting lover to her duke.

She sits across from me in our dining room. Her pale blue gown makes her eyes glow. Long, silvery blonde hair spills down her back. The heart-shaped neckline of her dress highlights the swells of her breasts. For some reason, they seem larger lately, and I'm not one to complain. I watch her finish her meal, her goblet of wine untouched. The image of her starving body will stay with me forever. As I take in the fullness of her face, I fill with happiness.

Leaning back in her chair, a secretive smile curves her lips.

Mischief gleams in her eyes as she stares across from me. The servants have been dismissed; I can tend to my wife's needs. We don't have an extensive staff anyway. My magic does most of what we need, and it's best if not too many people see me. I am not a human man. Scarlett and I have had enough rumors spread about us over the years that we don't need to add any more.

To the king's credit, he doesn't check on us very often. Last week was the first time he had stopped by in months. Once he was satisfied with how we were keeping the land, and even more pleased with the tithe we paid him, he was off.

I have no great love for the life of nobility. Taking care of our tenants and minimizing squabbles between farmers is tedious work. However, it is a small price to pay to keep Scarlett safe and happy. I would give anything to have her just as we are now.

I gave my soul to have another chance with her. Being a duke is nothing by comparison.

There are days when I still feel like that creature. My monstrous nature has never truly gone away. My need for my wife is a testament to that. I take her roughly—our lovemaking is primal to the point I've burned countless bed linens and tablecloths. We have dozens of replacements stored around Fog's Nest Manor. Additionally, I don't believe the maids are persuaded by tales of faulty candle usage anymore.

My wife's wicked grin stirs more heat to life inside me.

"What brings a smile to my darling wife's face tonight?"

"You know why, husband."

I have a few guesses. Especially when I can still feel her nail marks along my back and know she has my seed drying on her thighs. She had a nice dinner prepared for us tonight, that's why she insisted on dining formally. If it were up to me, I would've brought the feast to our bedroom to be enjoyed between bouts of lovemaking.

My desire for her never wanes—I dare say it's gotten worse over the past year.

Ever since I was a boy, I have admired her from afar. The earl's daughter with the shining hair and beautiful face. The one who was quick to laugh at my childish jokes or sought me out with day-old bread when I had gone hungry from the night before. I've loved her for as long as I can remember. It shocks me that she feels the same. Her adoration burns as hotly for me as mine does for her.

There isn't a day that passes that I'm not certain of our eternal love. It hums between us during quiet moments like this. Our bond is so intense sometimes I think I can see it dancing between us. We rarely get visitors, and that suits me just fine. I want my wife's sole attention, especially on a day like today.

Our anniversary. Technically, our second wedding, but the only one to be made official by a priest. The two of us married on Samhain—an ode to the old gods who blessed our hand-fasting. I had gifted Scarlett the sapphire necklace that decorates her delicate throat this evening. It had brought a smile to her face, and I had enjoyed it even more when it was the only thing she left on while I bent her over our bed.

She had said she had my gift with her and she would bestow it on me tonight. I could hardly wait.

"You're looking at me funny, my love."

Her soft voice sends all the blood rushing to my cock. It strains behind the lacings of my trousers, begging to find itself back in her tight pussy. I roughly adjust myself below the table and take a sip from my wine glass. Food tastes good again, but nothing will ever compare to Scarlett's incomparable sweetness.

"How am I looking at you?"

"Like you want to devour me whole."

"I do."

Color engulfs her cheeks as she reaches for her water glass and takes a small sip. After a moment, she rises in a swirl of pale, blue silk. Her eyes burn me alive.

"You seem eager for your gift, husband. Let me prepare it for you."

Scarlett rounds our dining table, trailing her fingers along the polished wood. Leaning down, I inhale her rose perfume and nearly come in my pants at the feel of her lips at my ear.

"Join me in our chambers in five minutes."

Her lips graze my cheek, and then she is gone, slipping through the oak doors with a high-pitched giggle. She loves to torment me, and I allow it. She's going to get it rough tonight—hell, she always does. She loves the primal way I take her. I seek her out at all hours of the day to relieve this desire for her. I would worry I was overstepping if she didn't take me with the same fervor.

I've been inside her in every room of this manor home we built atop the ruins of her former home. We christened it in love to wash away the stains of the past. Every hateful memory is wiped away. Those who came before us are not welcome here —not even as ghosts.

Finally, the wall on the clock shows five minutes have passed, and I hastily rise and leave the room. Portraits of Scarlett in various outfits and poses decorate the walls. There are some paintings of us together and of the house, but they are few and far between. This house is a testament to my devotion to her, and it is clear to all who enter who owns my heart.

Taking the steps two at a time, I rush down the carpeted hallway and burst into our bedroom.

My mouth goes dry at the sight of her. My seed threatens to spill without even a touch from her. Scarlett is a vision—too beautiful for words. Her eyes tell me she knows the effect she's having on me, my wonderful, wicked wife.

Atop the satin sheets of our bed, she is surrounded by gauzy red fabric. It spreads out around her in a crimson cloud. The material is not thick enough to conceal her. I can see every lovely dip and curve of her body. Her hard nipples poke through the red, and I nearly fall to my knees.

"I thought you deserved to unwrap something today," she purrs.

I nearly go out of my mind as I stumble towards her. She drifts up to me like an angel bestowing a dying man his final wish.

"You are my favorite thing."

I quickly shuck off my boots, while her hands go to my overcoat. The silver buttons hit the wooden floor with a thunk. Scarlett's warm palms slide up my sides under my undershirt, and I help her remove it. My pants go next, her breathing speeding up as my nakedness is revealed.

The proud length of my cock stands at attention. Milky seed beads at the tip and skim down the grooves along the side. Scarlett moans, and her thighs rub together. Crawling forward, she licks her lips before taking me in her hand.

Her tentative tongue snakes out to lick my seed from the tip. I groan, my head falling back on my shoulders. Scarlett licks me again while her fist pumps me roughly. My hands fall to her head as she sucks my length deep. Her tongue works me in and out of her hot mouth. The perfect tightness of her throat encourages my climax, but I withstand her torture.

I've come all over Scarlett throughout the years—marking every inch of her—but tonight I have the desire to spill inside her pussy. However, that doesn't mean I won't allow my wife to have her fun, especially when her teeth graze my shaft.

"Fuck," I snarl, gripping her hair. "You're too good at this."

"Thank you, husband," she murmurs demurely around my cock.

She works me extra quickly. Fisting me over and over until my teeth snap together. I can smell the delicious scent of her pussy. I'll need my tongue in their soon. Scarlett releases me with a pop. My seed mixes with her saliva and paints her gorgeous lips.

"Do you want to come in my mouth? Or on my tits?" She

bats her thick lashes at me. "You can put it anywhere, Krane. Wherever you want."

"Fuck, you're trying to kill me."

Her eyes turn innocent.

"I'm just trying to be a good wife for my husband. I want him to reward me with his come."

My vision blurs around the edges as she sucks me deep again. Her hand grazes my balls, and she gives me more teeth. My hips move of their own accord, fucking myself down her throat. Tears fall from her eyes as she chokes on my cock, sucking me harder. Her sloppy moans around my cock are nearly my undoing. Pleasure tingles along my spine, but I fight against it.

Releasing her hair, I pull out of her mouth and hook her under the arms. She gives a sound of protest, but I'm already wrestling with her covering. The fine fabric shreds in my hands. Her gasp is music to my ears.

"That was expensive," she condemns.

"I'll be you a hundred more. I need inside you. Now."

She rolls her eyes, but slides her legs open wide. Her glistening pussy calls to me. With her mouth on me, I'm crazed with lust. I need her deep. Pulling her from the bed, her legs go around my waist. I pin her to the nearest wall and hook my hands under her ass. Her arms go around my neck, and she holds on for dear life.

I thrust into her roughly, the first pump of my hips unmakes me. Her pussy is so wet and tight. I don't know how I'm going to last, but I will. Her breasts pillow between us, and I take her lips in a bruising kiss. She tastes of blackberry jam. Her moan is the only encouragement I need as I pull back and fuck her into the wall.

Our lower bodies slam together. The portraits along the walls rattle and shatter onto the floor. Scarlett screams into my mouth, her nails clawing at my back. We mark each other inside and out. She pulls my hair, makes me bleed, and I let my desire run rampant on her little cunt.

"Krane, I'm close," she warns.

Her pussy begins to quiver around me. The punishing rhythm is heightened by my hand that finds her clit. It only takes a few rough strokes for her to erupt. She clenches down on me and soaks me with her sweet come. I push deep, butting up against her womb, and emptying myself on a roar. Seed spills from her little hole and soaks her thighs.

Scarlett's eyes are dazed as I pull her from the wall. Her quivering body tucks into mine. Her mouth is open against my birthmark, trying to get her breathing under control. Our sweat-slick bodies slide together, basking in the moment. When I'm inside her, we are truly one. The afterwards is almost as good, this feeling of our souls knitting together.

Once she has come down from her peak, she rolls back onto the bed, her fingers staying on my birthmark. Something dances in her eyes—an emotion I haven't seen before.

"Do you want your gift now?"

I chuckle, taking her lips in a soft kiss.

"You're spoiling me. That was more than enough." I nip her throat. "Unless you want to let me fuck your ass again."

Scarlett laughs, pink decorating her cheeks.

"Later," she agrees.

"I don't need anything else, Scar. You're all I ever want."

Her smile turns secretive once more as she takes my hand in hers.

"Well, unfortunately, the gift I got you can't be returned."

She settles my palm onto her soft stomach. Tears fill her blue eyes, and for the first time in my life, I don't know what to say to Scarlett. My fingers tighten on her skin, my mouth falling open. Does she mean—surely not—she can't be—

"Are you sure?" I ask.

"The doctors confirmed it for me today. We're going to have a baby, Krane."

A howl rumbles from me as I collect her to my chest. Our laughter is watery as we share gentle kisses. A baby, truly. A family between Scarlett and me was something I always dreamed of. When I had been cursed, I thought there was a chance I had lost that dream too.

How wrong I had been about so many things.

"Are you happy?" she asks.

I kiss her soundly.

"Scarlett, you and this babe, and however many more we should have, will make me the luckiest creature in the world."

Kissing her again, I taste her salty tears.

"I love you, my sun."

"I love you, my moon. Always."

Everything we lived through brought us to this moment. All the longing—the pain and betrayals—none of it matters. When you find a love as consuming as mine and Scarlett's, you fight for it until the end. The past was dark and full of demons, but our future is brighter than ever.

This will be a new adventure for us both, and I can't wait to embark on it with her. Scarlett, the only girl I've ever loved. My wife. My soulmate. The one who's loved me as a boy, as a monster, and as whatever I am now. Our love can withstand anything.

Even death.

DON'T MISS THE NEXT ONE!

A treasure hunter seeking unimaginable wealth. A fairy queen intent on teaching him a lesson. One week in her realm will change both of them forever. Coming June 2026!

READ MY OTHER BOOKS!

Interconnected monster romance standalone on Kindle Unlimited!

Short and spicy monster romance novellas following a different diabolical looking creature!

ACKNOWLEDGMENTS

Thank you for picking up *Saved by the Headless Horseman*! I've never written a second chance romance before so I really hope you enjoyed it. I know this one was a bitter sadder than my other books, but I felt like their ending was perfectly sweet.

I'd like to thank my beta/ARC teams, my patrons, and all of you who've shared or continue to support my work. I'd love you even with a pumpkin for a head!

See you in the next one...where she'll be the monster!

xoxo Charlotte

ABOUT THE AUTHOR

Charlotte Swan is twenty-seven year old, living in Chicago. When she is not dreaming about being whisked away to a world filled with magic and sexy monsters, she is busy being a freelance social media marketer and full-time smut lover. To read her debut novel *Taken by the Dark Elf King*, hear about her upcoming projects, or to connect with her on social media please find her on her website or by scanning the code below.

www.authorcharlotteswan.com

www.ingramcontent.com/pod-product-compliance
Lightning Source LLC
Chambersburg PA
CBHW031538310726
48971CB00008B/2526